RAISE THE DEAD

A LOVE STORY

TONY FUENTES & C.S. KADING

SANDDANCER PUBLICATIONS

To everyone who has ever fallen in love unexpectedly.

Paperback ISBN: 979-8-9852825-5-9

Ebook ISBN: 979-8-9852825-4-2

Copyright file: TXu002341793

Cover and Chapter Headers by Etheric Designs

Necromist artwork by Tony Fuentes

Layout by Atticus

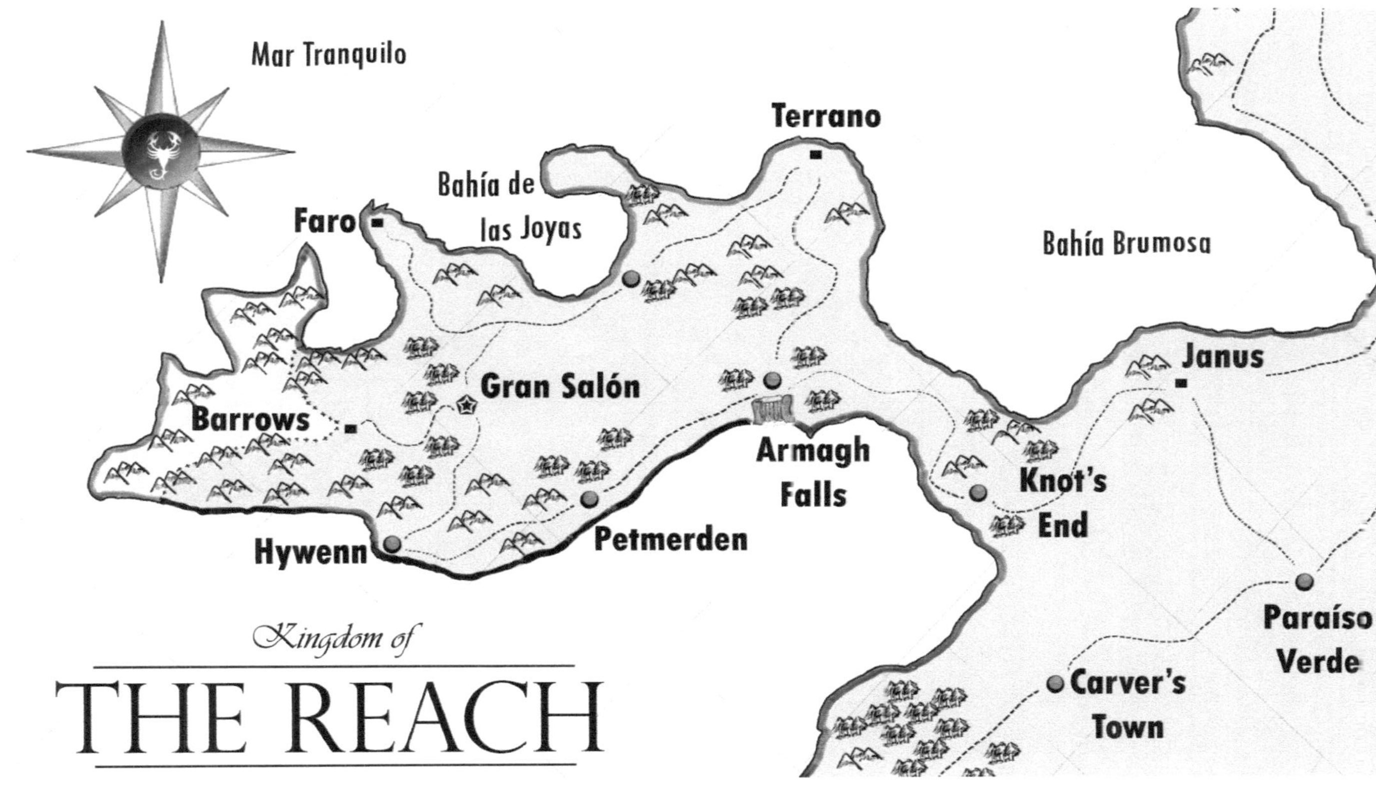

Mar Tranquilo
Terrano
Bahía de las Joyas
Faro
Bahía Brumosa
Barrows
Gran Salón
Janus
Armagh Falls
Knot's End
Hywenn
Petmerden
Paraíso Verde
Kingdom of
THE REACH
Carver's Town

CONTENTS

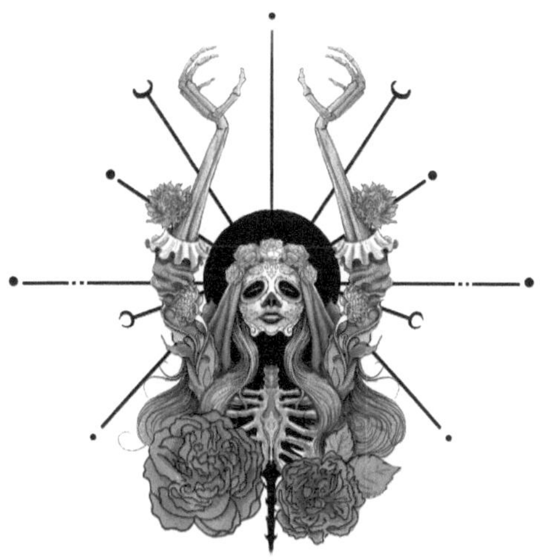

AN INCONVENIENT TRUTH

Emilio Kane stretched out on the table and looked around the dimly lit room. Normally, he would rest comfortably in his bed upstairs, but on a night like this, the workshop was the best place to be.

The summer months made it too damned hot to fall asleep. Even with all the windows open, there was not enough of a breeze to justify sleeping in his own bed. The idea of sleeping and sweating was unpleasant enough that he decided the workshop was the lesser of the two evils. The cellar beneath his house was originally meant for storage, but he had converted it to a workshop when he moved in long ago. The stone walls were excellent at keeping the air cool, but the large blocks of ice he had brought in regularly made the space a bit of paradise. However, the trade-off for sleeping down here meant he would have to fall asleep with the constant chatter all around him.

Kenzi Page was firing off questions to old man Hillard. While a patient man his entire life, Hillard wore the look of a man who was more than ready to meet his maker. Page was in her mid-twenties and wanted to know everything about Hillard and his life. Page had been trying to chronicle the kingdom's history and what better place to start than with one of its oldest citizens?

On the other side of the room, the Lawsons argued. It was not unusual and, in fact, based on the argument, tonight seemed a common occurrence. Hilde Lawson was lamenting the fact that Gerald still had not repaired the broken steps on the staircase. It had been a decade. Gerald fired back by citing that they shouldn't be sleeping upstairs at their age.

There were a few others as well, but they all soon became background noise. The conversation was certainly more pleasant than weeping and wailing. He found that the restless dead were always better in groups than as individuals. While they were still bound here for one thing or another, they found some solace in not being alone.

Emilio was a Necromist, one who deals with the dead. While trained in the mortuary arts, a Necromist, such as himself, could also see and speak with the dead. In doing so, he ensured that the shade would pass on from this world into the next, wherever that may be. Having the ability to discern accident from foul play, or provide real answers to questionable intentions was an invaluable talent to have. It also meant that he could hear the constant conversations of the dead until they moved on.

Unlike the living, the dead never rested.

Page had been killed because of a kick to the head from Hillard's horse. The poor animal reared up and kicked the chronicler when it realized that Hillard had died while seated upon its back. Nothing nefarious, simply old age. Hillard's heart had given out while Page had been interviewing the old man. Fate was funny that way.

The Lawsons "sort of" died in their sleep. Their neighbors had reported a strange smell coming from the Lawson house. A sewer line in their house had been repaired multiple times, presumably by Mr. Lawson. The most recent of those repairs was... hastily done... to put it politely. This quick repair had failed, and the air had gone foul, killing the couple in their sleep.

Taking off his shirt, Emilio rolled it up into a pillow and put it under his head. He contemplated running back upstairs for a proper pillow and a sheet, but the chill in the air allowed laziness to set in. He stretched and allowed his body to relax enough that he yawned deeply. That was a good sign that sleep would overtake him soon. Closing his eyes, he took a deep breath and let the conversations slowly fade into the background and into nothingness.

Something felt off. It suddenly became silent. None of the shades were talking. There was only the stillness of the night. Opening his eyes, he sat up and looked around the room. The surrounding shades had all fallen quiet and were bowing their heads in deference. Turning towards the stairwell, he saw her standing there.

Her face was proud, but not overly harsh. This was a face that commanded attention and gave direction. Something about her was strangely familiar, but he could not place it. It was strange for her to be here. Indeed, this shade should not be here at all. The eight shades in this room were present because they accompanied their eight corpses. The eight corpses that Emilio was preparing for their final rest. An untethered shade was always possible, of course, but never for a good reason.

Her pale eyes looked Emilio up and down as if searching for something. Scanning the rest of the room, she drew her gaze back to him and she finally spoke.

"Are you Emilio Kane?"

The dead rarely knew his name, which made this entire encounter even odder. Sliding off the table, he took a step forward, and recognition hit him like a sack of hammers.

"Yes, Your Majesty... I'm...my condolences on your passing?"

Marisol Failla, Queen of the Kingdom known as The Reach, was dead, and her ghost was standing in his workshop.

"There was no passing, Mr. Kane. I believe I have been murdered, and I need your help."

The Queen of The Reach had been murdered. This was going to be a long night.

The Reach was a smallish kingdom on the northern edge of the Imperium of Kraphax. Despite its small size, The Reach was known for being the only Kingdom in the Imperium that produced two of the most sought-after exports. Coffee and Cocoa Beans.

Nestled securely in the caldera valley of a long-extinct volcano, the rich, volcanic soil of The Reach provided the perfect bed for these two plants to grow in harmony with one another. The edges of the ancient volcano provided a buffer against coastal gales, allowing the storms to break upon their impressive barriers and provide gentle rains and freshwater runoff below. The southernmost side of the caldera had exploded some thousand years past, destroying everything around it. But, as nature is wont to do, fresh water and seed spreaders allowed the fertile land to produce vibrant life in the wake of utter destruction. Volcanic stone, spewed from the caldera's dramatic death, created a rough land bridge to the main continent from the caldera, like a child's hand grasping hold of its mother's apron, giving the area its name.

The Reach.

Isolated, but possessed of some of the richest farmlands in Kraphax, The Reach was wealthy and well cared for. The shining jewel of the Imperium.

King Raphael Eskil had been the sovereign of The Reach for the past two decades. His passing three summers ago had been upsetting for the whole Kingdom and sent shock waves through the Imperium. Nature abhors a vacuum. Politics doubly so.

Since King Raphael's death, The Reach had been governed by his son Lykos. Lykos had been groomed to be a leader ever since he was a child. He was capable and quick-witted. King Raphael of The Reach had been killed on a hunting trip when he was attacked by a wild boar, despite being warned of the animal's proximity. The attack had been quick and vicious, leaving no time for the King to react. In a last-ditch effort, the boar had ripped a large hunk of flesh from Raphael's neck, gouging out much of his throat. The King had bled out before the royal hunting party could get to him. Lykos had been inconsolable for weeks. Eventually, the young prince climbed out of his grief and took up the mantle, so abruptly forced upon him.

The first order of business thrust upon him was to reestablish alliances.

Marisol Failla had been that alliance.

A marriage between Lykos and Marisol had been arranged, a political marriage. Yet, from all reports, the couple had fallen in love. It was a rare thing, but it was not unheard of. That love, combined with King Raphael's years of shaping his son into a capable ruler, made Lykos Eskill a force to be reckoned with. Some whispered that he threatened the other nobles and that Lykos was far too powerful. Others said that he was simply a King that knew how to get his way, but he was careful and not overly ambitious.

Now Lykos' bride, the Queen of The Reach, stood in the cellar of a little-known Necromist.

Emilio rubbed the back of his neck and pondered the situation.

"Forgive me, Majesty, normally I would offer you refreshment but..." he gestured about.

The spirit of the late queen steepled her fingers together before her and rested them at her midline in a very regal pose. She watched Emilio silently from the foot of the stairs. Across the room, Kenzi Page leaned in to whisper something to Hillard. The old man nodded and replied in tones no one else could hear. They were stuck in their resolution loops even still. Until they had resolved the issues which bound them to this plane, they were condemned to remain. Emilio had planned to help them resolve their issues in the morning so their families could continue with their burials. He stared at the free-floating figure of the Queen. Plans were going to change.

"Is there some other place we can talk, Mr. Kane? Some place a bit less … crowded?" she said as she forced her gaze back to Emilio.

Remarkable! Emilio thought to himself. Typically, when someone was murdered, their spirits were struck by inconsolable grief or rage. The Queen seemed more… put out… than enraged or in despair.

"Oh! Well, you don't have to worry about them, Your Majesty. Shades are known for their discretion. Dead men tell n…" he stopped himself short and pursed his lips. "You know, on second thought… let's go to the formal office above, and we'll … sort this out?"

She appeared unhappy at the remark, but he couldn't have helped it. Working with the dead often drove one to find some sort of sanity in gallows humor. With what little professional dignity he had, Emilio gathered his shirt, slipped it on, and made his way upstairs. The shades returned to their conversations as if nothing had happened.

Back up in the hot night air, Emilio turned and saw that the Queen was lingering down below. He watched her for a moment before clearing his throat. "Your Majesty? Is there something wrong?"

She turned away from the scene in the workshop and made her way up the stairs, "Those people … they are all…"

"Dead, Your Majesty, yes. Either through old age or accident, but very much no longer... with us," he said as he caught himself. He was going to say the land of the living, but given the situation, he was not sure what might upset her.

"Why do they... and why don't I ..." she started.

Emilio expected questions. There were always questions. "All... well... most of your questions will be answered inside," he said as he motioned into the house. "While everyone else around here knows I can speak with the dead, very few folks are ... comfortable... with it. It gets them thinking about their mortality and reminds them of some of our... hmmm... troubling history. Rather than spook people, I try not to interact with the dead in public. Makes things...easier?"

While unnecessary, she took a deep breath and solemnly nodded her head. "I understand."

Following him inside, Marisol watched as the Necromist turned on the gaslights of a small office. The furnishings were nice, but not too extravagant. Most of the comfort was placed on the chairs and couches that filled the space. Designed for visitors and not for himself. Behind the desk was a rather modest chair with a thin cushion. It was clear that he placed more care on providing comfort for those in grief than for himself.

Settling in behind his desk, Emilio ran his hands through his hair to give it at least a semblance of professionalism. He slapped his cheeks a little to wake himself up. "Now, to answer about those shades downstairs..." he started.

"Shades?" she said as she raised an eyebrow.

"Right!" He nodded to himself and looked up at her once more. "Apologies. Work jargon. Let me explain. In the beginning, or rather should I say ... in the end... when we die, a few things can happen. Some folks die and they immediately move on to the next world or place. Depending on what god you follow or no god at all, you end up somewhere. Before you ask, no, I don't know. However, we can discuss it later, if you wish," he said with a slight smile.

It was a practiced smile designed for comfort, but it still felt genuine. It did not matter the person or the position, his place was to offer comfort in times of loss and sorrow. Such behaviors were expected of political dignitaries and political pawns. But Emilio was neither of these.

Marisol nodded simply and settled in the chair opposite his desk.

Seeing her sit down relaxed him a bit, but watching her engage with her surroundings also piqued his curiosity. Taking a moment, he looked at her - or rather, looked through her. Behind the facade of every Shade and Spirit was their essence - their Alma. To Emilio, the Alma displayed itself as a skeletal mask that bore the truth of one's character. Designs and flourishes often decorated these masks. Many did not know the full meaning of the designs on the faces of the dead. But these 'death marks' seemed to tell stories of how a person lived their life. The Queen's markings were both elegant, and strong. On her head was a crown of five vibrant flowers. He had not deciphered the meaning of the flowers. Shades and Spirits seemed to carry a random number, but there always seemed to be at least one. Curiosity satisfied, he smiled and nodded his head.

"So sometimes when people pass on, they simply move on to the next world, place, what have you. Then there are the souls downstairs in the workshop. Most of them died purely by accident. Their deaths happened so fast and quickly that they did not even register they were dead. The others died of natural causes. In both cases, these shades are still here because there is something unfinished from their lives that tethers them here. They died before something important to them could be completed. They have different names, depending on who you ask, or what lore you may have been taught. I call them 'Shades' because they are an echo of the person who once was. While a Necromist like myself can interact with them to find out what needs to be completed, if unattended, they fall back into the last moments of their lives. Mr. Karsen is still reading his book. The Lawsons are arguing and Ms. Page is firing off questions. Your sudden introduction into their patterns and you, being who you are, triggered that response."

The Queen nodded her head. He could tell she was taking it all in and accepting it.

"So when we left, they went back to what they were doing ... but do they remember us being there?" she asked.

Emilio's eyebrows bunched. They were entering territory that was rarely discussed outside those of his ilk. "That is hard to say. They are often very sharp about remembering everything up to the time of their death. Everything afterward can vary from shade to shade. I've had a few shades that remembered me. But I think it is only because they knew me before they passed on. Most treat every interaction as new, so I have to treat every time we talk as the first time, even though we may have spoken a dozen times already."

Marisol looked down at her hands for a moment. He could feel the question coming.

"Since I was not an accident or done in by natural causes, Mr. Kane, is this why I am ... different?" she spoke with some guarded hesitation.

Emilio regarded her features, searching them for information. A hint of purple tinged the aura that surrounded her ghostly figure, showing trepidation or fear. His eyes softened as he gazed upon her, longing to take her into his arms and offer her compassion and support in this time of confusion.

"Well, Your Majesty, those who have been murdered are a different lot. If someone is killed violently and they are aware of it happening, the energy surrounding that incident creates what we call a Spirit. Spirits are a copy of that person in life. They are exactly what they were while living, but like a Shade, they are here because of something profound and unfinished. Usually, it is their murder." Wiping the sweat from his brow, he reached over to the pitcher that sat on his desk and poured out a glass of water.

The water was room temperature, but it would serve its purpose. Clearing his throat, he left the glass untouched. It was time to ask the hard question, "So, given that you know you were murdered, Your Majesty, can you tell me who did this to you?"

Marisol considered the question for a moment. "I thought it was a dream at first... a nightmare. It was dark, darker than it should have been. The only light was creeping from around the door. I was lying in bed and I saw someone step out from behind my mirror. At first, I thought it was a trick of the light, but they walked toward me. They were...they had no face."

The Queen stood up and paced the room, recalling the moment. "One hand clamped down over my nose and mouth ... their other hand was at my throat. I tried to fight, but they were like a stone statue." Her voice seemed to get louder as she spoke. Turning to Emilio, she continued, "I tried! Gods, did I try! I screamed as hard as I could! I hit them with everything I had. I hit them as hard as I could! But it did nothing. I could do nothing!"

The air in the office suddenly felt cold. Emilio watched as the glass frosted up. This was the sign he was looking for. Those whose lives were taken from them had the possibility of becoming a Spirit but also depending on circumstances - something very dangerous. A Spirit, touched by anger could be consumed by it. Like a disease, the emotion could infect them, causing them to be warped by their rage. There were many names for these creatures. He had to ensure the Queen did not become one of them.

"YOUR Majesty ... LADY Failla ... Marisol?" he asked loudly. Saying her given name aloud, Emilio hoped it would throw her emotions off.

Marisol stopped mid-stride and gave him a curious look, followed by that of confusion. The room was covered in a fine layer of frost.

"What ... what happened?"

Again, he gave that comforting smile and motioned her to sit. "Emotions, especially those at our last moments, are powerful. They carry so much power that they can affect the physical world." He raised both his hands, and spoke with a cautious tone, "What I say now to you is with the utmost respect. The thing that killed you bore an unbridled rage. A rage that was so powerful that it bled into you at your moment of death. You need to maintain control over your rage. It was the emotion you died with, and it is a force of power within you." He ran his fingers over the fine frost on his desk and rubbed the thin ice between his fingers. "That rage can warp you. A Spirit is an amazing thing! YOU are amazing! An exact copy of who you used to be. You can learn, remember, and grow with those experiences. However, this is usually for only a short time. It is the job of someone like me to ensure that you complete what you need to do to move on. Whether it is completing some task or bringing your killer to justice. I am here to help."

Marisol's purple-tinged aura pulsed like a heartbeat. A faint red glow within her. He was right. There was something dark and red in that anger. Something he could not let her give into. She took another unneeded, deep breath and sat down with her eyes closed.

Emilio let out an inward sigh of relief. He had thought that perhaps a casual conversation would send her on her way. Had he known he was dealing with a murder, he would not have left his tools in the basement. The office afforded some protections, minimal warding, and the like. He was not prepared to deal with what was at hand. He had to keep her focused, and with any luck, she could move on before she became more dangerous. He needed her to remember without riling up the memories once again. He needed a different approach.

"While I know it is improper, may I call you Marisol?"

Opening her eyes, she looked up with a slight smirk. "I don't remember the last time anyone has ever called me by my name." She looked off to the side. "I don't think Lykos ever called me by my name. It was always, 'Dear' or 'My Queen'. It's a bit funny now that I think of it." She looked down at her lap and then nodded her head. "Yes, please call me Marisol."

He gave a small smile and nodded his head. A small victory. "Again, I don't mean to dredge this on for any longer than we need to, but you said the person who took your life had no face. Were they...masked or was it you could not see them?"

The red pulse flared for a moment within her, but quickly faded. He watched her close her eyes and remember.

"No, they didn't have a mask." she continued. "They were pale, like something that never knew the warmth of the sun. As they cut off my air, they changed." Marisol's brow furled, fighting to recall the moment despite the emotions that tried to cloud the memory. "They began to look like ... me? That last moment... it was me! A copy of me killed me?" Her eyes opened with confusion.

Emilio frowned.

"Not a copy. A doppelgänger. A doppelgänger murdered you and has taken your place. That means no one knows you are dead," he said.

When a human being is murdered by another, their Spirit or Shade can be bound to the murderer. When something outside of humanity kills - the metaphysical tether of guilt is snipped, and the restless dead roam free. Was she the only one or was she the first of many?

Things had just gone from bad to worse.

WHAT IF'S

There were very few professions available to someone who could see and speak with the dead. Most cities had ordinances against the presence of Necromists within their boundaries. Some villages both within The Reach and on the mainland drove them out of town entirely. Occasionally some poor fool would run up against a particularly close-minded group, still holding onto the fear of superstition, and their body would be found swinging from a tree.

The Imperium took no formal stance on the existence of those blessed or cursed with the ability to commune with the dead. The Imperator, of course, frowned on the murder of their subjects, but rarely sought justice for one that was wronged. Supposedly, the Imperator employed a necromist for the Royal Court. Someone whose very presence discouraged subtle political assassinations. Whether it was true, the thought of someone speaking with the murdered spirit and getting the truth of the matter discouraged such things. Differences of opinion that warranted such brutal address and political challenges were most often addressed through the practice of duels.

Some Necromists found employment as physicians who would oversee such challenges. Their purpose was to save a life, where possible. If not, they would quietly and discretely ensure the Spirit of the slain duelist found its final rest. Duelists were keen on paying extra to get the services of a Necromist in these cases. There were, of course, stories of unscrupulous Necromists allowing a Spirit to haunt those responsible for their demise, exacting in death, what they were denied in life.

Emilio did not seek to become a Necromist. It was not a calling that one pursued, or a set of skills that one opted to learn instead of, say, becoming a cobbler. One was born with the ability or not. He had been fortunate in that both of his parents were medical professionals. Neither given to the fear of the dead nor superstition.

Nonetheless, they kept his gifts secret from friends, family, and the community at large for as long as they could. He learned the medical arts from both of them and was encouraged to take up a mortician's shingle. He tended to the sick and ailing in their last days, and their families in the aftermath of their passing. In the privacy of the time of mourning, he also tended to the Shades of the departed and ensured they made their way to the next world. He would also occasionally work with medical students to ethically obtain cadavers for the operating theatre. That specific action frequently involved speaking with the new Shade and requesting consent for their body to be used in this matter.

There had been more than one occasion in his own time of study where an angry Spirit had taken up residence in the Operating Theatre, offended at what was being done to its former shell. Grave robbers, with the aid of unprincipled medical staff and morticians, had dug up the recently dead and dragged their bodies to the school. They did not know what they had brought with them.

As a medical student, Emilio studied the anatomy and physiology of many life forms. One started with small frogs, grasshoppers, and crayfish, and worked their way up to higher-order animals. Humans were not the only sapient life form in the Imperium, but it was a rarity to examine the remains of non-humans.

Emilio had seen a doppelgänger once. More correctly, the body of one. It had been a decade or more ago. One of the more renowned professors was giving a lecture on non-human biology. Emilio had secured admission to the lecture. The climax of the evening was the reveal of a doppelgänger caught and held in mid-transformation. The technique used to hold the creature was something well beyond Emilio's scope of knowledge or understanding. It was more than a simple taxidermy, that much was certain. Parts of the creature appeared indistinguishable from a normal human. Pores in the skin, bone structure, muscle density, and internal organs all mimicked what one expected

to find in the body of a deceased human male. The
rest of the body, however, resembled something akin to
a great cephalopod. It was surmised that this connection
allowed them to assume the shape of other creatures, as
many cephalopods possessed the ability to camouflage
themselves completely.

Regardless of the rest of the information presented
through the lecture that evening, one thing had stuck
with Emilio over everything else. The eyes of the creature.
Eyes dissolved rather quickly post-mortem. For this reason,
taxidermists replaced the eyes of dead creatures with glass
representations that simulate the approximation of what the
eye looked like in life. The eyes of this creature, however, did
not appear to be fashioned of glass and were filled with an
emotion the young necromist recognized all too well.

Rage.

Marisol frowned, though not at the thought of a
doppelgänger, rather she felt a tickle in her brain; a memory
trying to make its way through. Closing her eyes, she looked
back at the memory of her death. Looking up at the thing,
subtle features formed. She could feel a cold well of anger
stir, but instead of lingering on it, she went past the thought.
Something about them that...

"... it still has my body," she said as she opened up her eyes.

Emilio nodded, "Go on," motioning her to continue the thought.

"Doppelgängers need to be in the person's proximity they pass for. They need to re-establish the connection nightly to maintain the facade. The only issue... if the person is too far away, the ruse is revealed, or if the body rots..." she said, as she recited some lesson from an instructor from years past.

"The visual mimicry is copied over as well," Emilio added. Looking down at his desk, his gaze fell to his open appointment book. "Marisol... do you know how long you have been dead?"

Her brow furled as she stared at her hands and concentrated on the moment once again. "The moon always sits in view of my window. When it hides from the world, I light a candle to..." she paused. "I know it's childish, but I light it to keep the darkness at bay. That was when I knew things were off. The room was too dark when I woke up. The candle was out. The darkness... won?"

It was one thing to help console the living. You could do so with a simple touch of the hand. With the dead, the best thing you could do was talk. It worked well with the Shades, but Marisol was a Spirit. A soul untethered. Against his better judgment, he placed his hand on the desk toward her.

She looked at his hand, and then back at him. The gesture was not lost.

Since she had been in this state, she had walked through walls and people. She accidentally spooked a horse or two. The only creatures who seemed unafraid of her had been cats. She was never much of a cat person, which was a little ironic. They simply stared at her, acknowledged her presence, and then simply went back to what they were doing.

Marisol knew she could not physically touch Emilio in her current state. Instead, she simply put her hand next to his. "Thank you, Mr. Kane," she whispered.

He nodded, and slightly cocked his head in thought, "You said you light a candle when the moon is away." He stood and turned toward the small office window. Stretching his neck out, he looked toward the sky.

"What is it?" she asked.

Pulling himself back in, "I will preface this with the following ...time is different for you now. There is no more day or night, things simply are. If you were killed during the new moon, then it has been a few days, nearly a week. The moon is a full, waxing smile right now. Which is concerning."

She frowned again. "More concerning than having an after-death conversation with the Spirit of your murdered Queen?"

Emilio's shoulders rose and fell in a non-committal shrug. "Believe me when I say that this isn't my strangest moment, but it is up there." He offered a small smile, then glanced back at his calendar. "No, what I meant is that it's been almost a week." He walked back to his desk and stood staring at the calendar there. His right forefinger tapped absently. "If the doppelgänger killed you and was impersonating you, that means ... typically... a few days of chaos. Eventually... apologies for the candor... but your body's rot would become reflected in its form. The ruse would be over. Unless it has moved on to impersonate someone else. I mean - a week is a long time, but..."

"But what?"

He looked up from the calendar to her. "There has been no news. Everything has been business as usual. I mean... I'm outside of The Reach proper for obvious reasons, but I still know people at Gran Salón. Kalidah Chandra works there, right? She's Guard Captain? Over the last year or two, she's sent folks my way for help. When anything important happens that needs my services, she usually sends me a message. I am certain that if the Queen were discovered murdered, I would have been summoned to ...erm... ask ... you... what happened. "

Surprise rolled over Marisol's face. "You know Captain Chandra? How do you know the Captain of the Salón's Guard?"

Emilio shrugged once more. "Well, it was a few years ago. Her father had passed, and there were ... issues in her home. So next thing I know, Constable Jessup knocks on my door and explains that a friend of his was dealing with issues that seem to be up my alley. Without getting into too many personal details, I helped her father. It wasn't any of my business. She paid for the help and that was the end of that. It wasn't until a few folks she sent my way mentioned that she worked for the Hall; that was it."

The memory of Kalidah was there. Something far off in her mind's eye remembered her period of mourning. One of the very times she remembered her somber rather than stoic. She carried a sadness about her for a month, but like all loss, she saw it lessen. Marisol paused in thought. A Spirit noting the loss and grief in others, but what of herself? Kane was right. It was certainly strange.

She looked up to meet Kane's eyes, "Doppelgängers are usually creatures of chaos, agreed. But you have not heard of a single thing amiss, which makes this situation even more deadly. News and gossip run from Gran Salón like a river. Which could only mean that it is still impersonating me," she concluded.

"Not only that, it means that it has found a way to preserve your body," he added.

"Wait, they can do that!?" she said in shock.

Emilio shook his head, "No, not normally..." he said aloud. *Not without help... from someone like me.*

Raising his hand, "Your Majesty, Marisol, before we go any further into the 'what-ifs', I will need some sleep. If we spend all night guessing, it will make the trip that much harder tomorrow."

Raising an eyebrow, "Trip?" she asked.

"The only way to know if anything is going on is to go to Gran Salón itself. If we start first thing in the morning, we can make it in two days by coach," he answered.

"We are two days' ride from the Hall?!" she exclaimed and looked off to the side as if trying to recall the trip. Was it longer because she was traveling by foot? She only remembered traveling towards here... towards the light.

"Why is there a large blue light above this house, Mr. Kane?" she asked suddenly.

Emilio yawned but quickly covered his mouth, "Apologies. There is a long answer and a short answer. I promise to tell you the full answer to your question in the morning, but the short answer is this...it's magic." Standing up, he motioned to the couch. "While I know you cannot feel it, the night is still too warm to sleep, so I will go back down to where you found me. I assume at this point you know that sleep is no longer a thing for you, but if you wish to sit and wait, my house is yours. You'll be safe here."

Standing up, she gave him a simple nod. "Then I will find you in the morning, Mr. Kane."

Emilio gave a slight half bow, though it was more out of 'royalty reflex' than a voluntary motion. He took a step past her, and then paused, "Technically it's Doctor Kane, but Emilio will also do in a pinch," he added with a half smile.

"But what about the... others down there? Won't they keep you awake?" she asked.

He shrugged, "Sometimes, Marisol, I have to pretend I'm normal, so I hear nothing at all."

He gave her an odd smile before venturing down below into the workshop. Alone in a stranger's house would have typically resulted in no end of stress, but his invitation made it comforting. The journey from the Gran Salón to here had been full of anxiety and fear. The welcoming blue light that led her here, her only salve. The house was a way off from the nearest town, so it was just him, his work, and the night. *Such a lonely existence,* she thought to herself as she wandered through the small home.

There was the office, a simple bedroom with a small bed for one. The sheets were a mess. There was a stack of books sitting on a nearby nightstand. An even smaller kitchen with various bits of food and vegetables hanging neatly from the ceiling. In the main room, there were more books upon books that lined one wall, pictures, and some painted portraits on another. Some pictures and portraits were familiar, something in the eyes of a woman who may have been his mother, or maybe a grandmother or other relative. It was hard to say, as some images looked nothing like family relations. Then she realized all of them bore an age about them, both the images and the medium themselves. These were all persons who had passed on. Those who he knew, friends, family, loved ones all. Yet, among these, there was no space dedicated to someone special.

Who cares for the man who cares for the dead?

FRAYED KNOTS

She remembered staring at the moon's smiling face when suddenly she realized she was not alone. Emilio had come back upstairs mumbling something before heading into his bedroom, and out again. The sky had already begun changing colors from black to violet to blue. Soon that blue faded into a rich orange and eventually a glorious light as the sun broke over the horizon. Emilio was right. Time flowed differently, or rather, her perception of it had changed.

A bellow and loud moan soon interrupted the sun's rising. Rushing toward the sounds, she suddenly found herself outside only to discover the necromist standing near a well, holding a bucket. He was naked and soaking wet - presumably self-inflicted. For a man focused on scholarly pursuits and the medical arts, Emilio Kane was an exceptionally fit specimen. Perhaps his physique was because of his self-reliance on everything around him.

While he was far from the most handsome man she knew, he was not ugly. At the same time, he was someone who could blend in with a crowd. His smile added to his charm.

Emilio Kane was easy on the eyes. He was an average-sized man, with dark eyes and quiet eloquence. Marisol found herself fighting the urge to stare.

She had seen naked men before, but his body piqued her interest in a different way. He had a variety of scars on his body. Curious for a scholar and not a warrior. She was at once drawn to and repulsed by the sight of the naked necromist.

"... Oh..." escaped her lips before she could stop herself.

Immediately realizing he was not alone, Emilio shifted the bucket to his waist, "Um... good morning, Your Majesty... apologies. I needed a quick, uh, wash before we left. I saw you were admiring the...uh...sunrise and didn't want to disturb you." he fumbled over his words."Right...I'm going to go...and get dressed." He made his way back to the house, keeping the bucket at his waist to preserve the remnants of his dignity.

With the grace of a trained diplomat, Marisol simply looked away and off to the forest as he made his way to the house. It was not as if she had never seen the male form before. Lykos was quite pleasant to look upon. Of course, there were also her "youthful" years in Derma before she came to The Reach. A thought flitted briefly across the monarch's mind - the necromist was not a bad sight at dawn's first light.

With that thought tucked away, she turned back toward the house and caught sight of the dancing blue light above it. Even in the morning glow, its brilliant blue would not fade away in the sun's glory. Here, up close, something about it was...pleasant? Comforting? It just...was. She was going to have to ask him about it, as well as enquire if there was a way to get to Gran Salón a bit faster.

• • • ● ● • ● ● • • •

"This town at least tolerates my presence because they see the good I do past the history. I do not want to test that tolerance, Majesty," he replied.

"Trust me," Marisol said, "It will work. The Guild has its rules, and regardless of who an individual is, these rules *must be followed.*"

Emilio frowned. The walk to the town of Knot's End was only half an hour's travel. As they made their way down the path and into the larger clearing, they could see part of the road fenced off to keep the grazing livestock in their perspective lots. Past the long stretches of farmland, silhouettes of buildings in the distance came into view. The closer they got, the more the ambient sounds of civilization became louder. Life was alive and well at Knot's End. People were going about their business, setting up shop, preparing food, and loading and offloading various goods.

Ever polite, Emilio nodded his head and waved to those who offered it in kind. The necromist normally visited twice a month for a few things he could not obtain by himself from the forest or land. A local stream provided him with fish regularly, and rabbit snares were also beneficial. His small patch of land yielded turnips, carrots, and beans, besides the medicinal herbs he needed for his practice. But sometimes it was just easier to pay a butcher a few coins for a chicken or slab of meat. It wasn't laziness. Sometimes he just wanted to treat himself. All in all, his relationship with the town was simple. He minded his business, and they minded theirs. If there was an issue, he was more than happy to help, accepted payment, and let them be. While he had no reason to distrust Marisol, her instructions to him along the road seemed... a bit odd.

As instructed, he beelined for the Messenger's Station. By Imperial Decree, Kraphax sponsored the Messenger Guild. Whether by horse, cart, or foot, the Guild was empowered to travel throughout the lands of the Imperium, as well as into the neighboring regions to deliver missives. Depending on the messenger telling it, stories sometimes took on the guise of legend as they trekked through the lands outside the Imperium, delivering missives to all. Messengers were portrayed as brave, rugged, and even dangerous. Fighting monsters, man, and other strangeness to complete their charge.

These stories, while great, were not as accurate compared to the Brothers Five. Enik and Wils Five were the Guild's representatives for Knot's End. Wils was the older of the two, broad, bald, and a bit unfiltered. Wils was the one who made the treks outside of Knot's End to the other villages, towns, and outposts. If anything prevented him from doing his job, it did not prevent him for long. Enik was nothing like his brother. Quiet, soft-spoken, but with a memory that seemed to go back years rather than days. It was said he remembered every missive ever delivered out of Knot's End. Enik was the one who made the treks through the network of towns and villages within The Reach. If there was a faster way of getting to the Salón, it would be through him.

Facing the main road was a single sign above the door, a stylized Scorpion with the word 'Messenger' below it. The scorpion stood as the moniker of the Guild, for it was a creature that traveled quickly and was one not to be trifled with. Walking up to the small office that faced the main road, Emilio made his way inside and waited at the desk. Unseen, the Queen's spirit went through the desk and peered through the wall, and called back, "This one is sleeping, you may want to hit the bell."

Emilio looked at the silver service bell at the desk, then knocked loudly on its wooden surface and called out, "Hello! Mr. Five?"

Marisol scowled at his actions, but before she could comment, the back doors opened up. Wils Five stood up, looking partly awake and partly cross. Focusing on the lone person in the office, his mind awoke with realization, "Hey! Look who it is, the Death Speaker! Shouldn't you be passed out from a hard night doing whatever the hell you do with corpses?" The tone hid no contempt, and barely hid any sort of insinuation.

While the insult was not directed at Marisol, any flicker of admiration she had for this guild member was extinguished in an instant.

Emilio gave a forced smile. Most people in town were in two camps of thought regarding his calling. They either accepted his work or did not. Wils was of the latter, and he made no efforts to conceal it.

"The dead never sleep, Mr. Five, and eventually we all join them." Emilio kept the forced smile on his face. Both men stared at each other, neither willing to blink, much less back down. For Kane, this was not a show of bravado. He learned long ago that you don't back down from a bully, no matter what.

Just as tension seemed to rise, another person entered from the back, Enik Five. "It's too early to be tossing around heat, man. Dr. Kane is a customer like any other. Just ask the man what he needs so he can be on his way." Although it was still early morning, Enik's tone was tired. He had been up before dawn doing what needed to be done while his brother napped.

"Fine." Wils glowered. "What does Mr. Kane need from the Guild? A letter? A package? How can we assist you?" While the words were not hostile, the condescending tone rang loud and clear.

"I have a delivery for Laurel. Homemade soup," Emilio said with little emotion.

Both brothers tensed up and stared at the necromist. "Can you please say that again?" asked Enik.

Emilio swallowed whatever was in his mouth and repeated the phrase. "I have a delivery for Laurel. Homemade soup."

"Tell them it is Cold, " added a voice neither brother could hear.

"The soup is cold," Emilio added with a straight face. It sounded so stupid, but the effect was apparent in the eyes of both brothers. Marisol was right.

"Shit..." was all that Wils could say before heading out the back door.

Enik began rummaging through a ledger and then glanced back up at Kane. "We should be good to go in ten minutes, sir. Will that be okay?"

Trying hard to mask the shock, Emilio looked down at his bag as Marisol instructed him and simply said, "Yes."

Enik headed out the back doors like his brother. From the little window, Emilio and Marisol could see them work quickly to bring out a small two-person coach. They watched as Wils checked and double-checked the wheels and harnesses. Enik led two geldings fitted with blinders to the coach.

Emilio looked at Marisol, who had a smug expression on her face. "Care to share with the rest of the class?" he asked.

"Oh, now you believe state secrets?" she countered.

He sighed, "You were right, this was not a silly plan."

"See, was that so hard?" she said with a knowing smile. "Every kingdom has a set of pre-established code phrases. These phrases mean certain things to certain guilds. In this example, a *Delivery for Laurel* is code for a treaty, usually one meant to prevent the threat of violence or war. *Homemade Soup* means that it needs to be delivered to the royal representatives in a given territory. If it is *Cold* that means that the danger is imminent, so its delivery supersedes all other matters of state."

"So they believe they need to take me to Gran Salón to prevent war?" he asked with a bit of shock.

"It is not a false statement, Doctor. The information you carry may well prevent civil unrest at the hands of my murderer. Come. They will get us there by tomorrow, first light. You're welcome," she said and walked outside.

Still stunned, he shook his head. She was something else, a Queen indeed. Looking back at the desk, he stared at the small silver bell sitting there unattended. *Thievery is okay if it means survival,* he said to himself and slipped the little bell into his bag.

True to their word, the Brothers Five had the coach and horses ready in less than ten minutes. Carriage and coach travel was common enough in the Imperium. The Guild operated coach services throughout the realms. Besides persons of importance, goods and mail were also couriered. Riding a horse at speed from Knot's End might have made better sense if it were an important missive that needed immediate attention. However, in this case, discretion was called for. One could never tell by looking at the sleek guild coaches whether they contained important news or just a load of turnips needed at a festival. Transport was transport, and anyone with coin to spend could hire them.

Wils grumbled a little as he finished checking the straps on the harness, muttering under his breath about what the world was coming to, where a man like Emilio Kane was carrying a missive of importance.

Marisol scowled at the man's judgemental tones, even if they were not specifically directed at Emilio. She was irritated enough at being dead, but to witness such callousness to a servant of the Realm was simply appalling.

Enik tossed a bag up onto the driver's seat. The coach bounced a little, the springs whining with the sudden shock.

"Alright, Doc. Let's go. We'll change horses at Armagh Falls, grab a bundle of road chow from liragorn's to eat on the way, and hit Petmerden about nightfall. We'll change horses, grab food, get you a new driver there, and hang the coach lamps, to drive through the night. They will take you on to Hywen and then the Salón. There's a blanket in the coach, you can use it for a pillow." The younger of the two brothers seemed less judgemental of Emilio's calling.

"Thank you, Enik." Emilio nodded. He opened the door to the coach and stepped in.

Marisol settled in across from him, just as surely as if she were a physical being. She looked around the interior and over at Emilio.

"How..."

The sound of the reins snapping accompanied the sensation of the coach lurching forward. For a moment, Marisol's form felt pulled through the seat as if the vehicle were going to leave her behind. The next, she had rematerialized back in her seat across from Emilio. The regal demeanor she had displayed was momentarily shaken.

"I am so sorry, Your Majesty!" Emilio exclaimed. "I should have warned you..." He seemed a little sheepish.

"It seems there are many things I need to learn...or relearn...about this new state of existence," Marisol replied. She tugged at her sleeves, an obvious trait she had when living. "Tell me, Doctor, am I in danger of being left behind should we cross running water?" she asked.

"What? No. You aren't a Vampyre." Emilio replied.

Marisol cocked her head and raised an eyebrow.

"There are some aspects of superstition that hold with those persons outside the realm of the living."

"Go on."

It was dangerous to have a conversation with someone about these matters who was not a fellow student of the arts. Studying the dead, or the un-dying as they were frequently referred to, was not something that most people were comfortable with. That the things that go bump in the night were real creatures was troublesome enough. That there were scholars who actively studied these beings was disturbing to most. Discussing such subject matter openly could lead to an uncomfortable situation. Even worse, it could place him in a precarious light. Care was always practiced when these conversations happened.

"Alone with a spirit, in a two-person coach where no other ears could overhear seemed safe; Emilio caved to her request.

"You are truly interested?" he asked.

Marisol's face contorted into something resembling exasperation. "Doctor Kane, we are trapped with no one but ourselves to keep one another company for the next 18 hours. We have established that my current condition will exist for an unknown...possibly extensive... possibly brief... time, depending on what is being done with my physical form at the Salón. We can sit here in silence for those 18 hours, and marvel at the glory of The Reach's countryside, or..."

"Or?"

"You are a scholar, are you not?" she asked.

"Educate me."

THE HONEST DEAD

Emilio considered her words and then settled back into his chair. It was going to be a long enough journey. A conversation might be nice. Never mind the fact that Enik would think he was talking to the air.

"Alright then, why does Wils Five detest my existence?"

"Well, he is a…" she started, but narrowed her eyes, watching him. "It's not you, but what you represent?"

"Warm," he said simply.

"Outside of the staring contest in the office, you were not in any way offensive to him unless the existence of what you represent is reprehensible to him."

With a raised brow, Emilio nodded his head, "So, the question is, what is a Necromist?"

Leaning back, Marisol rubbed her temple with the tip of her index finger. "Necromists are sanctioned tenders of the departed. By decree, they may aid in the final rest of those souls who have passed on. In doing so, they provide peace to the living and the dead."

Emilio clapped his hand to his palm gently, "Top Marks. But that term was only coined during the second Imperator's reign. Less than a hundred years ago. What were they called before that?"

Marisol looked up to the roof of the coach, or rather past it, then her eyes widened in recognition. Staring at Emilio, she whispered one word, "Necromancer".

"And that is why Wils Five detests me so. The Five Family have been members of the Guild since its founding during the reign of the First Imperator. They were there during the Corpse Wars. It would not surprise me if his great-grandfather fought against the ancient Death Mages of the time. He, along with countless others, fought against those who used the dead against the living. His prejudice is justified. Horrors were committed."

"So you are fine with the sins of your forefathers' overshadowing the accomplishments of the now?" Marisol asked in a cutting tone.

Emilio paused, not expecting such a passionate reaction from the deceased monarch. "Well, no. But it is the truth of existence, Your Majesty. That hatred runs deep into the very roots of humanity itself. Dead things should stay dead, as the saying goes," he shrugged and continued, "So all I can do is to be polite and kind when the opportunity affords me such. Most look upon me as a modern-day Necromancer that is no doubt scheming to bring about the horrors of old. The details of who and what I am are well guarded for the protection of others, so that is all people have to go on. One encounter with a single Necromist will not change the minds of society at large. I understand this. But I will continue to try. I was born a Necromist. What else should I do? The alternatives are not acceptable."

The ghostly queen leaned forward and placed her hand over his. It would have been a warm gesture in life. "Necromists aren't evil, Dr. Kane. Wils Five is a product of the very prejudice that we strive to remove from The Reach. It saddens me to see the oldest Guild of them all still embracing such hate. It is a shame because the Necromists working today are honorable people who wish to relieve the suffering of the living and the dead."

"Given all that happened historically with my kind, I can understand why people are hard-pressed for tolerance. After the Corpse Wars, when a few people showed signs of being able to see the dead, they were killed instantly. The Inquisitors of Hil were very thorough and very effective. If it were not for the Third Imperator's firstborn son possessing the Sight, I probably would have been executed as well."

Marisol nodded her head and added, "Which led to the creation of the Fugue Academy."

The Third Imperator's son, Travaren, created The Fugue Academy to end the mindless slaughter of persons born with the gifts of the Ars Necromantia. Neither the Imperator, nor his wife, nor any in their lineage, had been so touched. Had it not been for Travaren's striking resemblance to his father, he may have been declared illegitimate and executed. But it was not the fault of the child, nor the child's parents that caused Travaren to be so born. It simply was. Nonetheless, he could not be allowed to take the Throne, and so instead, stepped aside and created The Fugue Academy. The creation of the Academy also allowed those in power to keep a close eye on those so gifted to ensure a repeat of the Corpse Wars never occurred again.

Emilio nodded. "Exactly. If it were not for that institution, humanity would be forced to deal with the dead in 'unhealthy' ways. Let me ask you, history-wise, do you remember how the Corpse Wars ended?"

"The easy version is that the Death Mages were defeated by the Imperator's forces and that was the end of that. To be honest, it was not something I delved into. While I know it was historically important, their threat is considered no more, a note for those who govern to keep an eye out for," Marisol said.

Nodding his head, "Honestly, what you know is what most people are taught. The truth of the matter was things got bad. Really bad. When you have an enemy who could slaughter the innocent and add them to their power base, it becomes less of a straight-up fight and more of a war of attrition. The event that changed the tides was a group of Necromancers offering themselves in service to the Imperator. They proposed a different tactic and became the fulcrum to shift the balance of the war. Their plan was not to raise the dead. Instead, they created a method to contest control over the dead during those battles. Shades, spirits, and ghouls can only be controlled by one master. By forcing a contest of wills, the dead became free. Many... if not most of those poor creatures... panicked when they realized what was happening to them, or became enraged at the horrible things they had been forced to do and turned on their former masters. It's what allowed the Imperial troops to seize control over many of the battles and ultimately kill the Death Mages."

Marisol's brow furrowed. "I had not heard that Necromancers were working for the Imperator. What happened to them?"

Looking down at the floor of the coach, "When the last of the Death Mages had been destroyed, the Imperator called for his Necromancers and had them all slain. He could not take the chance that the same power would tempt them."

"That...that is horrible! Why would..." she stopped herself and answered her own question. Ruling and governance meant making hard decisions. Sometimes terrible decisions to save the people at large. The death of a small group to prevent another war was unfortunately necessary. Wordlessly, she simply nodded her head.

They sat in silence for a few moments before Emilio continued. "The tragedy in their deaths was the fact that they were only academics...teachers and researchers. Scholars who only wanted to explore the question of life after death. While nothing was stopping them from becoming like the others, those men and women were not masters of the dead. Many of them died when they first joined the military forces because they did not possess the ability to control the dead, or could not stomach the idea of doing so. Much like any soldier in a live fire training situation, I suppose." he picked absently at a tuft on the seat then looked up to Marisol, "They sought to learn and understand the condition of death, as well as what lay beyond for the soul. They believed in these lands, and their Imperator, and forced themselves to persevere, despite it all. In the end... there were less than a dozen that survived, only to be executed for helping."

"How do you know all this?" she asked.

"The dead do not lie. The spirits of some of those scholarly Necromancers, unfortunately, are still there at the Academy. A first-generation Necromist named Eunice Fountains found them and brought them there. She spent her life recording their histories and stories. The Imperium requires the Fugue Academy to teach the history of the Corpse Wars. Fountains' addition helped us all understand more. Despite what happened, they were still willing to help. "

Marisol considered his words and the weight they carried. It was a lot to take in. She wondered if she would have made different decisions when she was alive if she had known the truth of these histories.

"There was a light over your home if I recall?" she asked, changing the subject.

"Ah." Emilio's brows knit together for a moment in thought. "Yes. The... hmm... beacon."

Marisol's eyebrows lifted toward her hairline.

"Think of it as a... metaphysical practitioner shingle... for the dead."

Marisol's face was blank for a long moment as if she were connecting some dots in her mind, waiting for it all to make sense. When she finally spoke, her tone was gentle.

"... and that was how I could locate you?"

Emilio nodded. "Yes, I suppose that would be accurate."

"And others... like me... can find you as well? Using the beacon?"

Emilio shifted a little uncomfortably in his seat, across from Marisol. Her assumption was not incorrect. Any shade, spirit, or other creature whose rest was not final could sense, if not see, the beacon that hung in the ether over his home. He had placed it there with purpose some time ago, hoping to help to settle any of the restless dead that still frequented the area. It had been successful. At least two drowning victims had been recovered from the local lake over the last several years, who might otherwise never have been found. One had been an accidental death. An older gentleman walking too close to the riverbank when it gave way beneath his feet. The other had been the victim of foul play, her body wrapped in heavy carpet and tossed from a rowboat in the center of the lake. A jealous paramour, seeking revenge. Lost souls who would have been condemned to wander the banks of the lake for eternity without his help.

Used in this fashion, the beacon was harmless and even beneficial. Yet that had not been why they were created originally...

"Magic is not... a common practice for Necromists, is it Dr. Kane?" Marisol inquired.

Taking off his glasses, Emilio gave a slow nod. "Correct. Magic of that type is largely considered rare or even..."

"... Forbidden," she finished with narrowed eyes.

"Correct. The practice of Necromancy and its associated magics are forbidden by many because they were used to enslave the souls of the dead and bring horror and terror to the living," he replied but held up his hands to her to pause what he knew was coming. "However, someone who understands the magics involved can change the original recipe to do something positive. The beacon above the house was created to not only draw the restless dead to its source, but its green flames would sap the will of those who can view it. It would make the dead easier to control."

She raised an eyebrow. "Your light is a bright blue."

"I changed the recipe so that the dead who can see it would be drawn to it, but it would not sap out their mental faculties," he said. "I changed it so those that could perceive it would find me. That way, I can figure out what needs to be done to help them."

"By rights, Dr. Kane, regardless of your intentions... you are practicing forbidden arts in a land that would gladly string you up or imprison you for the remaining years of your life. Even telling it to me, I would have to report it because otherwise, I would be guilty of endangering the well-being of the land. Now I'm not in any position to do so. Why tell me all of this?" she asked.

Honesty. The dead were always honest, he told himself, and he felt he had to be the same.

Looking her in the eyes, "Over time, I've acquired a few of these recipes and rituals. Each one I painstakingly researched and changed its elements of control. There are a few I know that are as written because even when you can speak with the dead, sometimes it isn't enough. Some need to be put down immediately to save people. Specters in all their variations, for instance, have to be bound and discorporated because of the damage they can do. However, such acts are taxing and dangerous to the user. The few times I have had to do so... it was to save others. So why am I admitting this? You asked and I have no reason to lie to those I'm trying to help. What I do, what I've learned, I do not do for power, just the preservation of life."

Marisol watched him as he spoke. Emilio did not shy away from his words or present any of the tells of someone hiding from the truth. She watched as his hand rubbed the top of his thigh. She recalled seeing the scars on his body from the morning. That one, in particular, was jagged and pink still. She wondered how much of himself did he give to his calling. What kind of environment created people like Emilio Kane, and why there were not more of them in the world? She remembered her father compared people like Kane to shooting stars. They were rare to catch sight of, but your world felt a bit better when you did.

PETMERDEN

True to his word, Enik Five got the coach to Armagh Falls as fast as the land would let them travel. Armagh Falls was a collection of massive waterfalls that provided most of the freshwater within The Reach. While there were various freshwater lakes and ponds, Armaghians created systems of ducts to support the natural waterways beneath the earth. It was said that the water from the falls was the reason that the crops tasted so much better in The Reach than anywhere else in the Imperium. Both passengers remarked on its beauty from the small window. Just as Emilio contemplated stepping outside the coach, Enik opened the door.

"Dr. Kane, sorry to disturb you, but because of the sensitive nature of the trip, I've been ordered by the local guild master to confirm a detail. No offense intended, but I have to ask, rabbit stew or lemon grass?"

Marisol could see the tension in Enik's posture. He was not comfortable with the situation. She surmised that Enik's older brother, Wils, would have no hesitation giving Kane the third degree. Enik wasn't like that and it showed.

"Tell him, neither. It's a peppered broth," she said.

Emilio looked at her and then the satchel, and then back to Enik, "It's a peppered broth."

There was a small sense of relief, but also grimness on his face. "Thank you, Dr. Kane. I'll let them know immediately. When I come back, I'll have food from Iiragorn's ready for you and we'll be off."

Watching as Enik left, "So I assume that the contents of the soup dictated something of specific importance?"

Marisol nodded. "The Reach is one of the most fertile lands within the Imperium. We are also on the edge of the Imperium's influence in the northwest. The Imperium bears several loose treaties with the Free Peoples of Kaxian. While they are not hostile as a nation, there have been misunderstandings in the past that led to a few minor conflicts. Diplomacy has settled many of these. Regardless, they are a people that Imperium monitors. If they caused your message, they would have been the rabbit stew."

Emilio considered her words as he fiddled with the latches on his satchel. His own home was more than a hundred miles from the Kaxian border, but he could understand why Enik would be concerned with his answer. He knew it was necessary, the need for coded language for important missives, but it all just seemed kind of silly. Yet there it was, simple, silly, effective, and brilliant.

"Then what was lemon grass?" he asked.

Marisol's lovely face grew dark. "For both our sakes, Dr. Kane, it's better that you did not know."

The seriousness of her face killed the curiosity he had, and instead, he just nodded. "Can I ask about peppered broth?"

"Violence or threat of conflict because of an assassination attempt. Given that it technically has already happened, I felt it was fitting," she said.

The coach shifted a little as they heard the horses being switched out. Enik opened the door again, this time with a covered basket. "Food is fresh and ready to go, Doctor. It's also made for road travel so you don't have to worry about spilling given that the road to Petmerden is a bit bumpy. You good to go?"

"Carry on, Mr. Fives," Emilio said as he accepted the basket. Within a few minutes, the coach lurched forward again, and they were off once more.

'Bumpy', was an apt statement as the road to Petmerden was carved into the rocky slopes of The Reach. Landslides often blocked the road to Petmerden during the wet season. Rocks and the winding pathway were the best way to describe it. At times they could see the mountainside within arm's reach, while at others they saw nothing but blue skies with the occasional bird flying by. The path itself was only wide enough for one cart at a time, so they had to stop when it was needed. With the driver being careful, they would often stop to let other carriages pass. If there was no traffic, the pace was faster, but not fast enough for Emilio's taste.

As for the food, it was good if a bit cold by the time he got to it. Still, it was well seasoned, and the addition of potatoes and carrots made it hearty. Emilio wasn't one for carrots most days, but it tasted much better than he was expecting.

The warmth of the summer afternoon faded as they hit the forest's edge and the sun's rays fell behind the horizon. They had been traveling all morning and afternoon. While the carriage was not intentionally uncomfortable by design, being forced to sit for hours on end on rough roads made Emilio's legs and back ache. Enik had mentioned they would be in Petmerden around nightfall. He would need to get out and stretch to be certain before taking on the overnight leg of their journey.

Emilio's gaze followed the skyline as he watched the sun's light fading in the distance. It would be dark soon.

"You are concerned about the coming darkness, Doctor?" the ghostly apparition of the queen asked.

"There are always concerns in the absence of light, Majesty," Emilio said. It was merely superstition that linked nighttime with his art. However, the inability to see in the dark was a source of fear in most civilizations. Harmless shadows of scarecrows in fields became terrifying nightmares stalking a town. Frogs' eyes, caught in the glow of a passing lamp, became strange lights along a river's edge. Wolves howling to their fellows sent chills up the spines of villagers, fearing they might be attacked unawares.

To be certain, some things walked the night that bore concern. But many of these adversaries also walked the land in the light of day. A rabid wolf was every bit as deadly at noon as it was at midnight, but under the cover of darkness, a villager seeing a creature with the water-sickness suddenly saw a lycanthrope. All thanks to fear.

The carriage rumbled to a stop, startling the doctor out of his thoughts. He looked to the Queen.

"We should be cautious. Just in case."

Marisol nodded. Enik hit the carriage's door.

"Petmerden, Doctor. This is where I leave you. Change of horses and driver. Take a rest, should take about twenty minutes." He opened the door and offered Emilio a small wooden token with the Guild sigil stamped on it. "You can grab something over at The Lampwick. Give this to them at the counter. They will know it is part of your fees with the Guild. The next leg will be overnight but should be smooth. You'll be at the Gran Salón by dawn. I'll fetch you when we are settled and ready."

The town of Petmerden was not a large one. A few dozen buildings were scattered around the forest's edge but were mostly hidden in the trees. A small road ran through it and a creek ran down the path, making for some pretty scenery. The town was mostly for the locals, not for most visitors, who had the Guild to ferry them around.

Emilio shook hands with the young man and stepped out into the night.

The air was cooler and the sounds of the forest were more prevalent. He could hear the songs of the insects and even the occasional owl. The tree branches waved in a slight breeze. The air smelled fresh and clean, but also carried an earthy scent to it. The doctor could smell the sweet scent of pine mingling with the odor of moss and decaying wood.

The lamp above the door to The Lampwick was lit, even this early in the evening. Emilio entered and was met with the smell of fresh bread and ale. It was a cozy pub, with a roaring fire in the hearth and a few locals heating some food over it.

"Drink, sir?" Emilio was greeted as soon as he stepped in by a woman who appeared to be the bartender.

"A tankard of Blackstead. Please." Emilio flashed the small token the Guild driver had given him.

"Of course, the driver gave you the stew token?" the woman smiled. "Please, follow me."

Emilio sat at a table and was soon handed a tankard of Blackstead. The brew was dark and as rich and thick as hot chocolate. It was a sweet beer that came only from a few villages in The Reach and was considered a delicacy.

Soon after Emilio finished the tankard, a plate of steaming hot stew was brought out.

"Your stew, Sir," the woman said, "Stay long at The Lampwick?"

Emilio shook his head. "No, change of horses and carrying through to Gran Salón."

The woman cocked her head in curiosity, then remembered the Guild token she had been paid with. Her eyes drifted to the black medical bag sitting at Emilio's feet and then back to his face. She nodded silently. "Understood," she said and turned to head back to the kitchen, then turned back. "You any good with a pistol ... Doctor?" she asked.

"What an odd question."

"Travelers have had some ... issues ... on the overnight between here and Gran Salón."

Emilio nodded and lifted his tankard to his lips, drinking as he considered her words. He wiped the edges of his mouth with his thumb. "Vandals? Raiders?" he asked.

"Wolves that walk on two feet."

"Lycanthropes?" Marisol commented from behind Emilio's left shoulder. He started slightly. "There haven't been shifters in these woods since I took the throne."

Emilio nodded and tucked into his stew. "There have been no shifters in The Reach since Queen Marisol's Coronation."

The woman shrugged. "Tell that to the three drivers we buried last month." And walked back into the kitchen.

Emilio considered her words as she walked away.

"Maybe I will."

Kayman Hurst was introduced to Emilio by Enik as part of the passenger handoff. He was older than Enik and bore a hardened edge that was honed by his occupation. Unlike Enik, Hurst was armed with both pistol and blade. While Enik was friendly in demeanor, Hurst was ... prepared. He made no small talk, save giving his estimation of when they would reach Gran Salón. Not wanting to question the driver, Emilio gave his thanks to Enik and Mr. Hurst and then made his way back into the coach.

"It cannot be Lycanthropes," Marisol said from across the way.

"No wanting to seem rude," he said quietly, "...but you were murdered by a doppelgänger. So the chance of the disease coming back is a possibility."

Begrudgingly, she nodded her head. "Point taken."

The coach lurched forward, and they were once again off. The road to Gran Salón was much wider once they broke free of the dense forest. The path would be more precarious after that, since most of the trip would be through the rolling hills and moors. The road itself was steady, but at certain speeds, the curves of the road coupled with the ever-present mists from the rich soil could easily lead to disaster.

"Given the hour, you'll forgive me if I rest my eyes for a while, your Majesty," he asked.

She gave a slight smile. "You have my permission to rest, Doctor."

Tapping his temple in thanks, Emilio allowed the rocking of the coach to lull him to sleep.

Marisol watched his form relax, and his features soften as sleep eventually overtook him. She thought about their conversation from earlier. He was a practicing Necromancer. No matter the motivations or technicalities, that very fact was cause for death in many parts of The Reach. Yet, he was nothing like the stories she had been raised with. He was friendly and not terribly off-putting. He did not carry a sinister look about him or skirt the truth. He was careful in his choice of words, true, but did not seem intentionally duplicitous. Dealing with diplomats, she knew that this could have easily been a mask, something easily rehearsed, but that did not feel right either.

Even his home was nothing like the tales and legends. There was no unsettling eldritch feel to his hearth. There were no jars of organs, body parts, or macabre decorations. There were no effigies or strange stains on the floor. It was a simple home with portraits and an office to comfort the bereaved. There were no wandering ghouls, or skeletal legions lurking around his house. The shades that currently lived there were not ghastly guardians on a tireless vigil. They were just people or rather used to be. They were simply souls he was trying to put to rest. Their bodies were cared for with both dignity and respect. Of all things, his workshop was ... tidy. It was the only word she could think of to describe it. The only real supernatural aspect was the blue flame that burned above it.

Letting herself relax, Marisol tried to recall everything up to this moment. She had escaped Gran Salón and the creature responsible for her demise. The details surrounding the affair were not terribly clear even now. She remembered fear, loss, and grief. Despite the horror and confusion of everything, there had been a distant sense of ... hope? She could not pinpoint the exact location, only a faint sense of direction that she had felt drawn toward. Then she remembered seeing it in the darkness. A lone star, sparkling in the darkness surrounding her. It was... comforting. It was the sole thing that offered comfort in madness that threatened to engulf her. A light at the end of the tunnel.

The blue light above Emilio Kane's home.

Gazing back toward him, she felt a knot of conflict tighten in her chest. He was a magician practicing a forbidden art. His polite and kind demeanor did not matter. Did it? There were magicians and sorcerers within The Reach and throughout the world. Many of whom were capable of wonders and destruction. They were rare, but not altogether unknown. Even the religions dedicated to the gods of the land had those who exhibited a talent for Theurgy, the divine magics. However, all these beings reviled Necromancy and its horrid practices.

As she considered the case of Emilio Kane, she recalled he never used the word 'spells'. He referred to his used of magic as 'recipes'. It was kind of absurd when she thought about it. He said he had changed the recipes as if he were a cook that would substitute one ingredient for another. However, he also admitted to knowing some that were 'as written', but cautioned about the danger in their use.

It was insane! This entire situation was completely insane. Yet here she was, a spirit, a victim of murder by a monster, now in the company of one who others believed to be even more monstrous. Never once did he claim to be a "good Necromancer". He simply justified his actions by helping others, by being a decent human being.

"There are many who could learn from your actions, Emilio Kane." she whispered in the darkness between them.

WOLVES ON TWO LEGS

Emilio felt himself slam into the opposite side of the coach as the world erupted into chaos all around him. Marisol was nowhere to be seen, and he could hear the horses squealing in panic.

"Doctor Kane! Are you alright?" said a voice outside the coach. It was Hurst.

"Awake. Alive. Nothing appears broken. What happened?" he said as he tried to reach for the door. Slowly opening it, he realized the problem. The road partially collapsed. The horses, while uninjured, were held tight by their tack. The coach was stuck at an awkward angle, one wheel was broken, and at the edge of the collapse. The other just spun slowly on its own. If the horses moved forward, the coach would roll forward, further into the hole trapping them.

"Someone dug into the road. This is a trap," Hurst said as he drew a pistol. "We've been having issues along this stretch. Not to alarm you, but there has been a rumor of ..."

"Lycanthropes ... I heard it mentioned at the Lampwick," Emilio added.

Hurst nodded his head. "The bodies they've recovered were savaged like a wild animal, but I don't think it was them. I don't think this is them either." Reaching into his jacket, he produced another pistol and held the butt of the firearm out to Emilio. "I need to unhitch the horses or we're never gonna get out of here. Keep an eye out. Man-wolf or not, there is something out there."

"Several somethings, in fact," Marisol said.

Emilio jumped and swung the pistol in the Queen's direction. It was sheer luck Hurst had already turned his back, or there may have been uncomfortable questions to answer.

A look of offended shock crossed Marisol's face, but Emilio silently motioned to Hurst.

Rolling her eyes, "Fine. We shall discuss the proper handling of pistols later. There are several voices coming up from behind us. It sounds like a mix of men and women. They're arguing, so it's hard to tell."

Turning in that direction, he closed his eyes and tried to listen. Hurst had quickly calmed the horses, but all he heard was their snorting and clicking. He could faintly make out arguing, and it was coming closer. It was filled with anger, but there was also sadness and distraught.

"Mr. Hurst," he said quietly, "I think we're about to have company."

"Sooner than you think good sir," said a strange voice. Turning towards Hurst, Emilio saw the glint of steel at the man's neck and another hand over his mouth. The steel was not a single knife, but four blades fashioned into a claw strapped to the assailant's hand. The blades were already biting into the driver's skin, letting small red droplets run down his neck. Behind Hurst was a figure with a rough fur hood that covered the upper part of his face. "Do yourself a favor and drop the pepperbox, and maybe you will buy this man some more time."

Without hesitation, the doctor slowly kneeled down and placed the weapon on the ground. "We have no valuables in the coach. I will give you the money that I have, but that is all there is."

The cacophony of angry voices that came up behind him had laughter mixed in. "Oh, we'll gladly take the money, good sir, but we'll also be taking the missives you plan on delivering as well."

Turning around, both Marisol and he watched a figure come from the darkness, dressed in the same fur-cloaked attire. "A little birdy mentioned the Guild was accommodating a messenger on this fine night. Traveling at night means that whatever is being carried is extremely important. And important also means valuable."

More interesting than the man himself was his company. All unintended. All were Shades. Among the dozen or so, three women, a man, and a teenager stood out. Their bodies were in a horrific state. Chests and faces were all torn to shreds, as if by wild animals. Despite the savagery, one could still make out their style of dress. It was the same as Mr. Hurst. They were Guild members. The others behind them were dressed in rotted finery but were in a further state of decay, far beyond any sort of recognition. One among them stood out from the rest. The teenage boy. His clothing was neither Guild associated nor remnants of finery. They were the simple clothes of a town's person, perhaps a farmer. His skull was partially collapsed from a head wound, and like the Guild members, his death was more recent.

All their angry words ceased when they saw Emilio. While they probably could not have put it into words in life, they recognized him for who he was and what he represented in death.

All at once, the adults began speaking about who they were. Tomas Castenada, Lisbeth Goman, Nema Foal, Lucía Castro. Their names went on and on. All were murdered at the hands of the man they surrounded. But the boy did not do this. His eyes locked on the fur-cloaked man and tears streamed down his face. This was not a gesture of anger or a cry for justice. This was sorrow.

Tuning from the cacophony of names being thrown at him by the dead, Emilio focused on the boy. "Who are you?" Emilio asked the boy.

"No one you ..." the man replied, but Necromist wasn't listening to him.

"My name is Donal," the boy said. "That's my brother Uther. His friend Deacon killed me because I didn't want my brother to join his scheme. I told him that my brother wasn't a criminal like him. He hit me and I fell back and hit my head. I started bleeding. When I threatened to tell my brother what he did, he grabbed a bigger rock and killed me."

"Hey stupid! Did you hit your head too hard on the landing? I said, retrieve your bag from the coach, or your driver's dead." Deacon shouted down at Emilio.

Looking back at the man, Emilio nodded his head and then spoke quietly to Marisol, "Preservation of life, remember?"

"What are you talking about?" she asked.

Reaching out with his left hand to the group above, Emilio muttered and move his fingers in the air. The soft words rang cold in the air. His fingers traced a sigil directed at the boy. His words sounded like thunder to the ears of the dead.

"Doctor Kane! What are you doing!?" Marisol shouted as she covered her ears.

Panic flooded across Deacon's face as he watched the Necromist. "What the hell are you!?"

The boy's form went rigid and floated down to Kane and entered Emilio's body. Falling to the ground, he began to pant. Then he slowly stood.

Eyes that were no longer mortal looked at Deacon, who was quickly making his way down to the hole. Turning away, Emilio-not-Emilio looked at the other man and spoke, but it was no longer his voice.

"Uther! It's me! Donal. Deacon killed me. Deacon has been killing people for years. I told him I didn't want this life for you and he hit me with a rock. I didn't run away. He left my body in a hollowed-out log by the bank. He did this to me! He's the reason I'm gone."

"Don ... Donal ... is that really you?" Uther said. Pushing Hurst to the ground, he strode forward toward Emilio.

Opening his arms toward the big man in an attempt at an embrace, Donal-Emilio was stopped short by Uther's massive hand that grabbed them by the neck, slamming them into the coach. "What is this? Who are you?! How do you know about my brother?"

"It's me, Uther," the voices pleaded. "Our sister got married two seasons ago. Her name is Aggie. You both loved mom's wild berry pie. She tried to make it once after mom died last year but burned it. We ate in anyways."

Uther's hand shook as tears began streaming down his face. "How...how do you know that?"

"It's me, Uther. Deacon killed me because I didn't want you to become like him. He killed me, so you would have no one else."

Releasing his hold on them, Uther turned his attention toward Deacon. "You said you had given Donal money to go see Aggie. You said you took care...took care of him." The big man's form shook with anger.

Deacon paused in step and shifted backward. "What are you talking about, man? I did! I sent him on his way! I paid the Guild to send him to your sister."

"He's lying! He has mom's locket in his pocket! He took it off me before he stuffed my body in the tree. He's a lying, murdering thief!" Donal-Emilio said.

The words riled up the other shades above the pit. They shouted angrily at Deacon. Marisol could do nothing but watch as everything played out.

"Look Uther... I would never do you wrong," Deacon said as he raised his hands up.

"Empty your pockets, Deacon," Uther said as he closed the distance, the bladed claw gripped tightly in his hand.

"It was an accident, Uther! The damn kid didn't under ..." Deacon didn't finish his words as Uther slammed the claw into his chest. Reaching into the dying man's pocket, Uther fished out a small golden locket. In a pain-filled bellow, Uther drove the claw deeper into Deacon's chest. Blood gurgled out of Deacon's mouth in a wordless reply as his body convulsed and then stopped moving.

"What...what happened?" Spirit Deacon said as he materialized and watched Uther throw down his lifeless body.

"You're dead now, Deacon," Marisol replied cooly, "And you're about to be judged."

"Wait what?" he started, when the hands from above grabbed him, dragging him upwards. He struggled in their grasp and screamed when he realized who was pulling him. The group of shades dragged him screaming into the darkness. Then there was silence.

Turning back, Marisol saw Uther on his knees, holding up Donal-Emilio.

"It's okay Uther … I'll be okay now. Find me and place me near mom," they said. "Be better, please. Always be better, it's what you asked of me. I'm now asking of you. Be better, Uther." Emilio's body pulsed with hazy blue light and Donal's form stood up out of the Necromist. The boy smiled at Marisol, and then back at Uther. He placed a hand on his brother and then faded away.

Emilio took a few deep breaths before sitting up and looking over to Marisol, "Preservation of life."

With the big man's help, the coach was righted and brought back on the road. While both a highwayman and complicit in the murder of his fellow Guild members, Hurst made no objection to the help given by Uther. Nor did he not stop him when Uther left to attend to Donal's body. His concern was solely focused on Doctor Kane. He now understood what his passenger was, and the events of the past hour had unsettled his worldview.

The only words he spoke were, "It's time to move on."

Resting quietly inside the coach, Emilio sat there sweating. The duration of the possession had been longer than he expected, but it was necessary. Not only had he prevented the deaths of the driver and himself, but he also brought rest and justice to the souls who were denied such. Yet Marisol continued to stare at him from across the way. Her face was stoic and without emotion. If she was angry, disappointed, horrified, or everything all at once, it was impossible to discern. Attempting to break the silence, he moved to speak, but she quickly cut him off.

"Rest, Doctor Kane, you need it," Marisol said. No emotion marked her words.

Resigned, Emilio nodded his head and leaned back into the corner of the coach, and attempted to sleep once again.

GRAN SALÓN

S leep came in fits and starts as the carriage made its way
from Petmarden to Gran Salón. Emilio was accustomed
to sleeping in uncomfortable positions and locations. As a
medical student, and during his time at the Fugue Academy,
one slept when and where one could. Hours were long and
students did not always have the time or energy to traverse
the campus back to their dorms and sleep in their assigned
beds. Some students at the Academy even attempted to
sleep in the drawers in the morgue. This choice proved poor
for many of them. Spirits of the restless dead nagged the
sleeping necromists unendingly. These attempts resulted in
students who were often more tired than when they made
their ill-conceived attempts.

All save Emilio.

Emilio always found peace sleeping in the cold, dark,
cramped drawers. The spirits left him to his own as he rested.
The mortician screamed like a schoolchild the morning he
pulled the drawer out and Emilio was still there. Peacefully

snoring away, oblivious to the class that had assembled for the morning lecture and autopsy.

The embarrassed necromist was quick to gather his gear and offer apologies as he headed for his morning rounds.

"How?" was all they asked.

He paused in the doorway, confused by the question.

"I listened to them. Don't you?"

There had been a brief inquiry after that. Emilio's posting in the class had been moved up several steps, because of his almost innate understanding of death. His actions had opened doors for himself but also earned some enmity from his fellows at Fugue who felt upstaged by the awkward scholar from The Reach.

He could have had his choice of postings, but returned home and hung his shingle alongside his mother's, content to provide solace and care for the people outside of the city's influence. His father had passed on while Emilio was still attending Fugue. Too much heavy food and too few evening strolls with Mother and the dogs. He was a physician. He knew better. But he also loved his salted meat and oatmeal stout. He was a good man. Emilio could never replace the elder Dr. Kane, but he could not leave his mother to care for the estate on her own. Above all else, the main reason was his father's last request. Words that his mother would never hear, from father to son, as he drew his last breath and his soul slipped from his mortal form.

"Take care of her, son. She has no one else."

He would have done so without being asked, but the last wish of a dying soul made it even more important. With that, he was bound to honor it, lest his father's soul haunt the land, angry and unfulfilled.

Letters from Gran Salón arrived periodically, offering Emilio a position in the Capital. One or two bore the sigil of the Recruitment Officer for the Guard. There had even been one from the Academy, offering him a posting there as an instructor.

They went without being answered.

He'd set his mother's soul to rest two summers past, happy to see them finally reunited in a way that only one with his gifts would know.

Emilio looked out the carriage window as the gates of the capital approached in dawn's first light and wondered where this path would take him now. The capital had several names, depending on who you asked. Historically, it was referred to as Qando. This was the name that the Imperium gave it when The Reach was annexed some three hundred years ago and was the name that was printed on the maps. Before that, it bore two different names, each given by the ruling people of the area at the time. In each of these, the translation was the same.

Gran Salón.

The Great Hall.

The people of The Reach were practical people. They were farmers and craftspeople. Cultivators of some of the richest land in the whole Imperium. The community grew up around their shared space. A place where families gathered, told stories, mended shoes, crafted tools, and planned harvests. This Gran Salón provided warmth and security in times of need, as well as joy and memories in times of celebration. It only made sense that they would name the center of their small kingdom after the center of their community.

Gran Salón was like Knot's End. There was simply more of it. More buildings with more floors, more people, and more voices broke the silence of the morning. Putting his glasses on, Emilio looked across the way to see Marisol staring out the window. Even translucent, the morning light caught enough of her features that he forgot about the sounds and the chaos all around him. Stories had been penned to her as being both kind and fair as a monarch. Yet looking at her, it was not so much in her actions, but reflected in her face as well. He saw a myriad of emotions flicker across her eyes as she viewed the sights outside the carriage windows. There was hurt, longing, memory, nostalgia, happiness, sadness, sorrow, and joy. The full range of human emotions encompassed in just her expression. She was amazing, and yet so much more.

Quietly, he sat up and ran his hand through his hair. He was not sure how he should approach her now. Drawing down a possession was a very unsightly tool in his arsenal. It was not one he used often. It was draining to both himself and the soul involved. Worse yet, if he were to choose the wrong soul, it may cause a battle for his own. Stories of necromancers of old losing such battles of will to even more powerful spirits were an object lesson for a reason.

Despite the caution warranted, sometimes it was necessary. He thought back to the figure of the young boy from the night before. That spirit was still present because he had been murdered. He was a soul crying out for justice. Not merely for himself, but for his brother as well.

"We are a few minutes away, Doctor. Do you have a plan in mind?" Marisol said, without looking at him. Her attention was still focused outside, focused on home, her home.

Her words pulled Emilio from his thoughts. "Oh!" he considered a moment, "I figure that once we get there, I can request an audience with Captain Chandra, and try to … discreetly… explain to her the situation?" he said. "Though…honestly, we may play it by ear."

Marisol nodded her head. "I see."

He noted the distance in her reply and stared at his hands for a moment.

"About yesterday … last night. I had to do what I did because …" he fumbled over the words, "It was the only chance I had to give that boy a voice. Any other method would have involved an animal sacrifice … which I'm not too keen on, and really was not an opportune moment to do so. The things I did, what I know …"

"Were for the preservation of life. Yes, I know Doctor Kane. You have said as much. Though I am wondering how much of the Ars Necromantia you possess. What I saw and felt last night was not the work of an unpracticed novice. That was someone who understood the use of arcane power and its utilization. Such power and knowledge would make anyone uneasy - living or dead," she said sharply.

Emilio winced slightly at the sting of her words. Part of him wanted to continue the conversation, but any good graces he had from her at this point needed to be saved. She was upset at the display of necromantic power. Whether it was her living self that was displeased or her spirit self that took issue, he could not be certain.

The living only saw the faint glow of eldritch light and heard the two voices speaking at one. The dead felt the weight and power of his words boom over them like a church bell being rung. Emilio's eyes slid carefully over to the rigid figure of the Queen as she continued to stare out the window.

Trust had become a fragile commodity.

"Those phrases are a matter of state security!" Kalidah Chandra barked. They stood a good foot taller than Emilio, forcing him to look up as she towered above him. Kitted up in well-used but cared for armor, the Captain of the Gran Salón was a force of nature and will. Both of which exerted their presence on Emilio at the moment.

"Those words are held to the highest order of secrecy by the regional monarchs and the Guild! They are not to be used for anything short of a NATIONAL EMERGENCY! How you got those code phrases and WHY you used them better have come with an explanation to please the Gods!" Kalidah hissed. She was a terrifying figure standing atop the steps to the Salón.

There had been no need to send a messenger to alert the Captain of the Guard. She and a fully armed retinue met the Guild carriage at the gate. This early in the morning, there was no one else in the area. It had been by design. To ensure a message of importance would not create curiosity, and to help ensure the safety of the messenger and their missive.

Much to Kalidah's surprise, out of the coach came not a diplomat, agent of the Crown, or emissary of the Imperium. No, out of the coach emerged the gangly, rumpled form of Emilio Kane. Her anger at this was palpable.

"You have EXACTLY 30 seconds to tell me why I should not have you locked away and interrogated for theft of state secrets," she said.

She turned back to the dozen armed guards and made a quick gesture. They nodded as one and dispersed back to their normal stations. The gesture and the look that accompanied it spoke volumes. The Captain was going to handle this personally.

"Uh ... well ... you see." Emilio stammered. "Have... have you seen anything strange lately? Like with her Majesty ..."

he started, "... have you noticed that she has been acting strange or being more secretive than usual?"

Captain Chandra's eyebrows raised and her features tightened, "Fifteen seconds Death Speaker..." she said in darkened tone.

"I'm not sure how to say this ... but ... the Queen is not the Queen. She's been murdered and there is a monster running around in her place?" he pushed the words out even as he could feel the weight of her scrutiny bear down on him.

"Her Majesty is alive and well, Kane. So much in good spirits that she has been planning the Harvest Festival," Chandra said.

"The nerve of that creature!" Marisol said.

Emilio shot Marisol a look of help as he motioned to the Captain.

Marisol shrugged, "Play it by ear." she repeated Emilio's words back at him.

His brow furrowed at her smugness, "I am trying to help you, you know," and turned back to look at Kalidah. "Captain. Would you believe me if I told you that the spirit of your Queen is standing next to me? That she has been murdered and is being impersonated by a creature who is currently deciding which fall colors to use for the Gran Salón's archways?"

Chandra's eyes narrowed, and she looked to the spot where she saw his eyes wander, then back to the Necromist.

"Are you telling me you have a 'friend' with you who claims that she is Sovereign of The Reach?"

Before Emilio could answer, Chandra turned toward that same space and spoke in a quiet, but harsh voice, "Listen, you stupidly lost soul. Whoever you think you are, you have stepped way beyond the bounds of kindness and decency. Obviously, you are taking advantage of this poor idiot's well-meaning intentions because if you were the real Queen, you would know an impersonator would never get past our watch! You do not deserve the kindness one of his kind provides. Perhaps the Inquisitors of Hil would be better to secure your Final Rest!"

The mention of the Inquisitors lit a spark in Emilio's eyes. Something that neither Kalidah nor Marisol had seen.

Anger.

"Those savage murdering bastards are the very reason my job is so much more difficult. They don't bring a soul to rest. They antagonize it to the point of madness! And they wonder why so many souls wreak havoc on the…"

With a harsher tone, Chandra's finger snapped out and pressed into Emilio's chest, "Enough Kane! The Inquisitors bear more credibility than a backwoods Death Speaker! Tell your spirit to give their name now and I won't have to bring them in…"

From the corner of his eye, Emilio saw Marisol walk forward, speaking slowly. The words seemed… familiar. Then the weight of horror and surprise hit him. She was repeating the possession chant.

"No Marisol... don't do..."

Marisol stepped smoothly into Emilio's body, stopping him at mid-sentence. A wave of disorientation caught them off guard as their minds merged, causing Emilio to fall forward. Chandra reached forward to catch them.

"Thank you, Captain," Marisol-Emilio said, as their voices overlapped one another.

Kalidah released the figure of Emilio Kane and pulled away slightly.

"I apologize for the situation, but this was the only way." Marisol-Emilio continued. They reached to brush off their pants and slowly stood. "Doctor Kane is indeed telling the truth. Exactly one week ago, a doppelgänger slipped into the Gran Salón and murdered me. It's taken me that amount of time to find my way to this man's home and figure out what has been done to me. He has been kind enough to lead me back here and try to put a stop to whatever this thing intends to do."

While slightly unnerved by the two voices coming out of Emilio, Kalidah pressed, "That is a fantastic sounding story, *your Majesty*," she said with a bit of disdain. "Tell me this. What do I hate the most?"

"Besides having your time wasted," Marisol-Emilio replied, "Well let's start with you hate Markus's goat stew because you've complained it was too greasy or too tough.

You hate it because of the...digestive issues it gives you. Or that you love and hate red wine. Mostly because the last time you and I shared two bottles, I spent a portion of the evening holding your hair back as the contents of your stomach decided enough was enough. You passed out on the couch of the royal bedroom when Lykos was visiting the Terrano Outposts to the north."

Chandra's face was a mixture of shock, horror, and embarrassment. "Your...your Majesty? How...how is this possible? I just saw you an hour ago at breakfast. You can't be dead! How?"

Marisol-Emilio reached out gently and held her forearm. "I'm so sorry, Kalidah. This is not your fault. We are ... we are... what's happening..." they said and suddenly their eyes rolled back as their legs gave out.

Once more, Chandra reached out to catch the falling figure of the necromist.

Marisol found herself violently ejected out of Emilio and landed on the road, approximately ten feet from her former host.

Coming to his own senses, Emilio looked up and saw the panicked look on Chandra's face. Forcing down his bile, and urging himself upright, he looked around. Marisol was lying on the ground. Not moving.

"Marisol!" Scrambling down the steps, he began intoning another chant. If it were not in the light of day, Chandra or any other passerby would have seen his body glow with a slight blue hue. Kneeling quickly, he gently reached under the ghostly figure of the queen and lifted her up.

Chandra watched as the necromist knelt and appeared to scoop up an armful of ... nothing. He turned back to face her, arms held out in some strange pantomime.

"Please Captain, is there a place we can talk quietly?" Kane urged.

Chandra looked around and then back at Emilio, "Come inside and say nothing!" Turning on her heel, she walked away from the gate and inside with the Necromist in tow. The Captain made a motion, and the gate to the Gran Salón opened.

Marisol murmured something, but Emilio simply nodded his head and whispered, "It will be alright. I promise." and followed the Captain of the Guard past the gates and inside.

STRAINED RELATIONSHIPS

"**I**f anyone walks in on this, they are going to think I have lost my mind," Kalidah muttered to herself.

Across the room from her, Emilio knelt next to a small divan, upon which rested … air. At least that was all Kalidah could see. The necromist assured her that the ghostly figure of Queen Marisol lay on the divan, resting and apparently in poor condition. Irritation nagged at the back of her mind. Irritation and a feeling that she should do something at this moment. If Emilio's words were true, then the Queen had been assassinated, and someone … some … thing … was impersonating her. It placed the whole Salón under threat of harm.

She pinched the bridge of her nose and rubbed it, hoping the headache that was named Emilio Kane might lessen.

"Are there any of Hil's Inquisitors in the Salón at this time, Kal?" Emilio asked quietly.

She shook her head. "No, not for months. Do you need one?"

"Seven Hells no!" he replied. "I just need to be certain that she will be safe." Kane reached out and slid his fingers across Marisol's forehead. She moaned slightly. It was audible. Kane's eyebrows lifted in surprise.

Chandra's pose stiffened, and her head snapped in the sound direction.

"Was that her? What are you doing to her, Kane?!" she crossed the space of the room in three steps and towered over the necromist.

Emilio winced slightly at Chandra's tone, but made no sign that he was going to move. "Ministering, Kalidah. Have some faith ... please." His words were the gentle words of a healer, soothing, kind, and filled with compassion.

Kalidah scoffed and folded her arms across her chest.

"She shouldn't have done what she did out there," Emilio said, distress in his eyes.

"What exactly did she do?" Chandra scowled.

Kane leaned back and rested on his heels as his eyes continued searching the Queen's prone figure. "Hrm, hard to describe..." he offered.

"Try." Chandra insisted.

"Always so demanding," he quipped, not changing his focus from the Queen.

"Then you should not be surprised." Came the reply.

"Touche'. We … ran into an issue on the road from Petmerden."

"Lycanthropes?"

"Worse - humans driven by greed. They were vandals in wolf skins playing the part, and adding to the fear. "

Once more the Captain assumed an aggressive posture, though less directed at the doctor. "They attacked a Guild Emissary?! Were they the ones that have been responsible for the missing carriages?"

Emilio reached over to open his medical bag and began rummaging through its contents. "Yes. And Yes. But they have been dealt with... Captain. Mr. Hurst can give you the details." He explained as he continued to rummage. "Ah!" he recovered a small monocle fashioned of purple-hued glass. Placing the monocle to his left eye, he contorted his face several times until it sat snugly in his eye socket against his eye.

Chandra scowled at Emilio's actions and explanation, her distaste for his calling clear. "Was Her Majesty part of the resolution?"

"Of course not!" the necromist exclaimed. "Her Grace is still freshly dead. Such impassioned actions may corrupt her soul irrevocably!"

Kalidah rubbed her face with her hands in her exasperation. "I am losing my patience with you, Emilio."

"Yes, well, some things never change." He replied, and turned his attention back to where Marisol lay. Closing his right eye, he opened his left and gazed upon her through the glass of the purple monocle. Her resting form was outlined in a blue hue. In the center of her form, where a heart would have resided when she was living, a faint light pulsed. Slowly.

Emilio inhaled sharply. "Oh, no."

Chandra leaned over him once more. "What? What is it? What's wrong?"

"No.No.No.No." The monocle popped out of Emilio's eye and clattered to the floor. He scrambled up onto the divan, taking Marisol's head into his hands. "She watched me allow a young man's soul into my body to speak to the living and tell them what had happened."

Kalidah's expression soured. She made a gesture to ward off evil.

"Those gestures are completely useless unless powered by Theurgy," Kane said. He looked down at Marisol's face. To Emilio, she appeared resting. Sleeping. At peace. The light of her soul, the consciousness that tied her to the material world, and made her who she was, was fading.

The necromist watched the gentle lines on Marisol's sleeping face. If he did nothing, the possibility existed that she might pass from this world and on to the next. Peacefully. But the death of her physical form had been violent. It was possible that she would not go on to the next realm and return a Haunt instead. A creature intent on vengeance and destruction, devoid of compassion or rational thought. An entity he would have no choice but to destroy in order to save innocent lives.

"I cannot allow you to come to a violent end twice," he whispered.

Turning back to Chandra, "She witnessed a possession" he said simply.

Chandra bristled at the comment, "Excuse me?"

Emilio turned his attention back to Marisol. His eyes searched her features. "Allowing a Spirit to speak through oneself is a taxing endeavor, even for someone like me. It is not something done on a whim, Kalidah, I assure you. It was a last-ditch effort that helped turn what could have been a deadly situation into a victory. I... perhaps... used a bit of arcane magic to allow it to happen."

The Captain's demeanor darkened noticeably at that.

Emilio continued, " Mari ... the Queen must have seen what I did and .. somehow... miraculous woman that she is ... retained enough of it to mimic it. A spirit should NOT be able to use any sort of magic." He marveled at the ghostly figure before him, "But ... she did to me what I did to save our lives on the road. The difference is... I am alive, and she is not. I can rest and recover. She must have unwittingly used part of her own being ... her essence ... to allow for it to happen. Doing so has almost destroyed her, and if I do not act now, it will." the necromist looked back to the big woman towering above him, "I'm asking - as my friend, will you grant me two favors."

"I'm listening," Chandra said, her arms crossed.

"Allow me to perform a rite to allow her to stabilize. Think of it like a blood transfusion… just not blood," he asked.

Chandra's eyebrow twitched. The two had known each other briefly in their youth, before his assignment to Fugue, before he became what he was now. And it had been out of that familiarity and trust that she had called on him when her father had passed. But this was magic, and magic was dangerous. What Emilio was suggesting was profane. Yet, if what Emilio said was true…if Queen Marisol really was laying there, and she could be saved…

"Fine … do what you need to."

"Thank you," Emilio said quickly. "Second, I need you to witness what I'm doing."

Kalidah's eyes drifted to the purple monocle on the floor.

Emilio shook his head. "Not that easy. I wish it were. Using a different tool, I can allow you to see the dead as I see them, but only until the sun rises again. What I do, I do for her and this kingdom. I do not want anyone saying I did anything untoward to her while she is in my care. May I do so?" he asked gently.

Chandra gritted her teeth. She wanted to scream and throw Emilio's ass out in the middle of a busy street. Employing magic in her presence was one thing. Performing magic on her person was another. However, his reason was unfortunately sound. "What EXACTLY are you going to do, and what will it do to me?"

Emilio gently let Marisol's head rest on the pillow at the end of the divan and reached for his bag once more. He rummaged around quickly and produced a small jar.

"This salve… you lightly smear it below your eyes. I will say a few words and then you will see what I see until the sun rises. That's it. If you want to hear what the dead say, I can …"

"No!" Chandra exclaimed and snatched the small jar out of Emilio's hand. "Bearing witness is all I need to do. And it's all I want to be a part of. Get on with it," she said hurriedly.

She had fought raiders, crazed berserkers, assassins, and death cultists. She had battled monsters of horrible, violent countenance. Yet, the idea of viewing what lay beyond death's door shook her core. Chandra said she did not trust Emilio, but this was not entirely true. They had known each other for years. He had never caused her direct harm. He and his family had always been both kind and generous. Emilio never had cause to lie to her, but he skirted the full truth in many things. Perhaps it was for her benefit or for his own protection. Perhaps it involved his calling. It did not matter. The uncertainty of truth that existed was enough to shake any foundation for a solid friendship. Yet the lack of blatant betrayal also gave rise to occasional faith.

He gestured for her to hand the jar back to him and stood up slowly. Opening the small jar, he ran the tip of his finger across the viscous contents and then sealed it shut once more.

"Please look up. I don't want to get this IN your eyes, only under them."

Chandra obliged and Emilio gently reached over and ran his finger under both of her eyes while whispering some odd-sounding words. She blinked and could feel her eyes slightly tear up, and then ... nothing. The salve smelled floral, but she could not place it. She blinked again and looked at Kane and then moved her gaze to the divan.

Marisol looked like she was sleeping, but her form was not whole. She was transparent, unbreathing, and still. She looked as if she had been laid out in the state. Chandra tried to focus her eyes on the figure of the Queen and noticed that her transparency seemed to thin. It was as if she was literally fading away.

"Mari..." was the only thing she could say as pain and hurt washed over her. Clenching her fist, she turned to Emilio, "Save her, NOW!"

Quickly nodding his head, Emilio turned his attention back to Marisol. He reached into his bag once again and took out a wax crayon. Grabbing a candle from Chandra's desk, he lit it, then began running the blackened beeswax pastel through the flame. When it began to drip, he drew symbols into the palm of his left hand. Kalidah watched him wince as the heat from the hot wax burned his skin. She wanted to do something. However, not knowing what the necromist was doing, or whether her help might be a detriment, she could not take the risk. All she could do was watch as the strange man she let into her life burned his hand in order to save her Queen, her friend.

Once the wax marking was complete, Emilio chanted softly over the strange sigils on his hand. Black wax waves pulsed with a bluish hue, then Kalidah saw something pulse in Emilio's chest. The pulsing was red, a deeper, richer red than blood. She watched as the pulse ran from his heart, down his arm to his hand. The deep red mixed with the blue infused the symbols, creating a strange purplish light.

He whispered as he reached to place his forearm alongside Marisol's, "What I do is to save a life…"

There was a strange crackle in the air as their arms touched. Kalidah could see the pulsing purple light drift onto Marisol's arm like droplets of wine splashing into a glass of water. Tendrils of light ran like shooting stars throughout her form. For the briefest of moments, she saw the faint outline of Marisol's heart. It pulsed purple and then slowly beat in tandem with Emilio's. Beating in time with each other, she watched as her Queen's form became less transparent, and more whole. More Marisol. The pulse of the light was almost hypnotic and Chandra felt her eyes drawn to the strange transference that was occurring before her.

Marisol stirred and slowly opened her eyes, fixing on the features of the awkwardly handsome necromist, staring down at her. "Emilio? Where am I?"

Emilio smiled, then his eyes rolled up into the back of his head and he fell off the divan.

The hypnotic beat was broken. Kalidah blinked, shaking her mind free of the surrounding magics. Emilio lay collapsed in a heap by the side of the ghost of the Queen. Reaching for him, she realized he was covered in sweat and a lock of his dark hair had gone pure white.

"What the in the Hells did you do to yourself, Emilio?!" she said, pulling him up into a sitting position and leaning his back against the edge of the divan.

Rubbing his face, Emilio murmured two words, "... unexpected ... rest ..." and fell forward once more into unconsciousness.

"Dammit! Gods, I hate magic!" Chandra swore. Grabbing his medical bag, she laid Emilio down on the floor and placed the bag under his head. Turning back to the divan, she saw Marisol looking at her, a look of bittersweet happiness was all over her face.

"Your eyes are glowing, Kalidah," Marisol said, but for Chandra, there was no sound. She knew her Queen had spoken, but she could not hear her. Now she wished she had allowed Kane to do whatever he had offered, but it was too late.

It took Marisol a moment to realize that she could be seen but not heard. Pausing, she moved her fingers and hands and she conveyed a message that required no magic.

Kalidah understood the gestures. They were part of her training. While they would not carry an entire conversation, they shared enough. *You. Well?*

Every noble and ruling house bore its own hand signals for silent communication to warn of danger or to pass along quiet messages. While it was not perfect, it allowed Marisol to converse with her friend as much as the stunted communication allowed.

She shrugged slightly at the comment and gestured to herself.

Kalidah's face betrayed her sorrow at the comment.

Danger here? Marisol asked.

Kalidah shook her head, *No.* She gestured to Emilio's unconscious form. *Must report in.*

Understood.

Kalidah nodded, *You stay. Return soon.*

My thanks Marisol motioned and bowed her head.

My Queen she motioned back with a bowed head, *Watch him. Trouble.* She pointed to Kane on the floor.

Marisol saluted dutifully, but smiled with a bit of sadness as the Captain departed, locking the door behind her as she left.

HOMECOMING

She was home. She silently wondered if one could still call a place home when they were deceased. It was probably a philosophical conversation to have with Emilio at a later date. She looked at his sleeping form as she sat on the divan. The white lock of hair that had been absent earlier in the day stood out. A witch's mark. That's what they called it. She was certain he would hate that nomenclature.

Regardless, it was evidence of magic having been used. Magic that had marked his form for all to see. Something he would not find easy to hide in the days going forward. It was a symbol of its price on the user.

"What did you do, you silly fool?" Reaching out, she cautiously placed her hand over his to touch him. Her fingers did not pass through his. They felt almost solid.

Trying to think about what had happened earlier, she faintly remembered him picking her up. Was he stronger than he appeared, or did her spirit form simply weigh so little? How he did so was probably another one of his unspoken 'trade' secrets.

Necromancy.

He was risking much to help her. If it were discovered he possessed any true talent for the arcane beyond the simple gifts of sight and speech, it could mean an instant death sentence. Yet, despite this risk, he continued to lend aid.

"Your heart is too big, you caring idiot, you know that?" she said to his sleeping form and gripped his hand lightly. Did he go to such lengths for others she wondered?

The light in the room dimmed. She stood to gaze out the window. The sun was blocked by the clouds that arrived overhead. The bright light of midday sun was now a light gray. She reached out to feel the air, but there was nothing. The feel of the promise of rain was absent, as was any other sensation. She pulled back and rubbed her hands together, seeking a sensation. She could feel herself. That was something, at least.

Her eyes fell on her wedding band. In death, it remained on her finger.

"Lykos."

Longing hit her as she caressed the band. He was here. Somewhere on the grounds, he was here. She glanced back at Emilio, sleeping on the floor, his medical bag tucked under his head. Her eyes raised toward the door. She did not need a key to open it, she could pass through it. The Salón was hers to roam, if she so chose. She looked back to Emilio.

He would be safe here, she thought. No one would barge into Chandra's office unannounced, and if they did, Chandra could explain his presence.

This was her home. Her home... her husband. Marisol needed them both.

Settling herself into her determination, she turned and went through the door and out into the courtyard. The gray skies overhead had darkened. The light of midday felt like late evening. Surveying the area, she identified the house staff, guards, and other administrators making their way in and out of the Hall.

The idea of rain was less a promise and more of an eventuality, and they all knew it. Shutters were pulled closed, bright canopies dropped to prepare for incoming wind and storm. She searched the movement of bodies, yearning for a singular figure. But Lykos was not among them.

Where was he?

An unexpected moment of anxiety washed over her. She needed to find him. Another step away from Chandra's office. It would be fine. She would be gone for a bit. Two more steps. She would be back before they missed her.

Lykos.

She needed to see him. She MUST see him.

The Audience Chamber was built to accommodate 500 hundred bodies, tables, and chairs. It was used for daily business by the city's administrators, who often used the space to work in tandem with their Majesties on the day-to-day. The day was cut short because of rain. No one wanted to wait in the rain for a meeting with the King, and Lykos would always accommodate.

Now, with the removal of furniture and rugs, it was a large room with two very large hearths on either side and their thrones at the far end.

It seemed so empty.

Walking the length of the empty hall to the center of the room, Marisol felt a small sense of unease.

It will pass when you see Lykos. She told herself.

The light in both hearths had dimmed down to a quiet red smolder. It was summer. Their heat was not needed at present, but the light was welcome, as was the light from the gas lamps around the room.

Marisol scanned the room, searching. The only occupant now was a lone guardsman by the far door.

Think, think, think. Where would he be?

Pulling on memories, she recalled that on rainy days, Lykos would either be in his study or perusing the larder if he missed lunch. Making her way toward the study, Marisol caught movement in the corner of her eye. Turning, she realized the guardsman had assumed a position of formal attention. Looking around, she saw they were still alone.

Can he see me?

Walking toward the guardsman, she noted several things were out of place. The guard's uniform was not current. It was tattered and bore the sigil of King Raphael. She set these observations aside as she looked at his face. His flesh had tightened across his face and his eyes were sunken black pits. His lips were all but gone, leaving a rictus grin.

Seeing her approach, the guard saluted, "Your Majesty."

The instincts of the living would have screamed at her to run from this apparition. But something of her new existence gave her pause. Protectors of the Salón pledged an oath of service. One that required their service until their death. Some took their vows to heart and remained on duty until their final days, their last breaths standing their posts in the Salón.

The individual before her must be one of these. One whose oath held him here. Someone who had been rewarded for his service by being buried in the crypts below was a family member. Yet, here he was, even in death, a shade maintaining his post.

Admirable. But also sad.

She recalled Emilio mentioning that shades such as these were often held in place until he figured out how to help them move on. She considered for a moment. What would Emilio do in this case?

Addressing the shade, "Guardsmen, our apologies, but I have forgotten your name."

The guard turned to address the Queen. "No apologies necessary, Ma'am. There are many of us, and we cannot expect their Majesties to recall every single one given the matters of state." he said. His voice sounded hollow, but still carried a sense of respect In tone. "My name is Tanner," he said with a bow of his head, "what is your will?"

"Was his Majesty here for the afternoon briefing?" she asked.

"He was indeed Ma'am. The change in weather prompted the close of business, so he is in 'session' with house staff in the kitchen."

Lunch. He is at lunch.

"My thanks, Tanner. You have served your post well." She said.

There was a sense of satisfaction and relief from the shade. How long had he been here? Perhaps her words were enough? She would ask Emilio later, but for now, she knew where Lykos was.

Leaving the Audience Hall, she made her way to the kitchen. Voices echoed off the halls, carrying the back and forth of a conversation. As she readied herself to step through the door, she felt a chill run up her spine as she heard a laugh. Her own laugh.

The doppelgänger was in there.

As the conversation continued, she pushed her way through the door and peered into the room.

A massive table occupied most of the room. Around it were set several simple carved wooden benches for the staff. Markus's back was toward the door as he leaned on the table in front of him. A spread of food was laid out before them all.

Plates filled with a selection of food were placed before each of those seated.

On one side of the table, she saw Kalidah nodding while gnawing on a carrot. Beside her was Liam Stack, the Head of House Staff. Across from them was Marta Boyorquez, City Chancellor, and Tegan Light, Treasurer. At the head of the table across from Markus sat Lykos...and the Queen.

"...I'm sure Their Majesties will agree that confining the festivities just to the Hall may limit the amount of attendees, as few can make the trek," Marta continued. They were cut off by the soft-spoken Tegan.

"Which would provide a significant drain on the city's financial resources, with no guarantee of an increase in funds to replenish what is spent," they said.

"Tegan, this isn't a business... it's a party," Lykos said with a smile. "We have this same argument every year, my friend. And each year, the Salón maintains itself."

Marisol sighed. She missed his voice and smile. His attempts at charm in Council. Her eyes lingered on his face and form. His strong features were accented by the stubble on his unshaven face. He was being lazy again. She wanted to run to him, to hold him, to tell him she was right there. Her yearning was broken by Tegan's persistence.

"That isn't the point, Majesty? If there comes a day when we have a hard need for funds... what if it isn't there?" Tegan said.

The creature that was not Marisol spoke, "I agree with Marta on this, my King. The people need to enjoy the fruits of their labors." She reached down and picked a berry from the plate before her. "I am doing all I can to ensure that the Salón is warm and inviting." She glanced in Markus' direction. "I am certain that even poor Markus here would enjoy some extra hands to help with Night's Feast. By bringing in those extra people, we also increase goodwill and add a little coin in their pocket. Goodwill, while not tangible, is still a worthy investment, isn't it, Tegan?"

Tegan sighed and nodded. "Of course, your Majesty. But it IS my job to ensure that we maintain our level of prosperity. These last few years have allowed us this level of financial security, but I still have to be cautious. That is my nature and the nature of this job."

Marisol continued to watch the Queen as she spoke. All her mannerisms, her posture, and her voice, were mimicked. She was a perfect copy.

"Be nice to Tegan, dear. They are just doing their job." Lykos chuckled. He reached across the table and took the creature's hand in his, then lifted it to his lips and kissed her fingers.

A slow fire burned in the pit of Marisol's stomach.

The Queen smiled as she continued eating the berry. At first, Marisol thought she was looking at Markus, but then realized she was looking at her. She knew she was there! Her eyes were glowing, just like Kalidah's.

Marisol backed toward the door and away from the Council. The slow fire in her stomach churned to ice.

The creature smiled as she bit into the berry.

"Of course, my love."

She ran.

Doors and walls, once barriers and guides, were meaningless now. Lights flickered or extinguished as she flew past them, driven by pain. Window sills were coated with a rime of ice that faded in the stone's warmth. Running through walls and rooms, Marisol found herself outside in the courtyard. Her emotions were awash with anger, horror, and anguish.

The thunder cracked above, and the dark gray clouds released their burden on the world below. She turned her face to the heavens and fell to her knees as the rain came down. She wanted to cry; she wanted her hot angry tears to run down her face and mix with the cold rain as it ran down her face.

But there was nothing, and no tears fell.

There were no tears at the moment of her death, and so there were no tears to call upon in undeath. She was denied even that.

The Queen's laughter - that THING'S LAUGHTER rang in her head.

"STOP!" she roared to the sky. Red darkness boiled in her chest, threatening to consume her. Fear, heartache, and loss swelled against the rage of the undying, preventing it from gaining a foothold.

She let her shoulders droop and her head fall forward. She was tired of this nightmare. Tired of all of it. She was so tired. She just wanted it to end.

"Ma'am?" said a strange voice above her.

The voice pulled Marisol from her grief. She looked up. Three guardsmen stood around her. One held a buckler over her head, to shield her from the rain. They, like her, were no longer part of the land of the living. She glanced at the heraldry on their livery. One wore Lykos' sigil, the others bore emblems of long-gone monarchs and regencies. Even in death, they stood as protectors of the Crown.

How many of them still walked these grounds?

The one who spoke to her seemed familiar, but she could not place his face. She stared up into his sunken features.

"My Lady?" His milky eyes filled with concern for her as he offered her his hand.

Marisol reached for his offered hand and accepted the aid. She felt a supporting hand on her elbow as she rose. Such tenderness and care, even in death.

"My apologies, good sirs. The pressures of…" she began, but stopped herself. There was no need for lies.

The dead never lie. Emilio's words echoed in her memory.

"Forgive me, gentlemen. All of this ... has been a lot to take in. This new existence...this death...all of it. I needed a moment of release. To let it out. I apologize if my demeanor was less than it should have been."

The two 'older' guards nodded their heads and saluted. Spinning on heels, they walked back to their original places along the wall and resumed their patrols.

The younger guard remained at her side, still holding his small shield dutifully over her head.

He nodded, "My...wife." he paused at the word as if trying to recall a memory attached to it, "My wife used to say screaming clears the soul. She said that if you hold things in, it hardens you, and hurts you more than helps. We also deserve to scream, Ma'am. No crime in that - crown or not."

She listened to his words of comfort and nodded at their wisdom. She wondered at the Shade's interactions with her. Her bellow of frustration and the threat of Rage must have broken them from the echoes of their routines and called them to her side. Guardsmen to the last, they rushed to the aid of their Queen even now. Another philosophical debate for another time.

"Shall I escort you inside, Majesty?"

"No, Guardsman. Thank you for your kindness."

"It is my honor, Majesty," he replied as he lowered his shield. Saluting, he resumed his post.

Marisol closed her eyes and let the rain fall on and around her. She stood tall then and took a deep breath, letting her mind imagine the scent of water on the stone and the chill on her skin.

She would not let this thing win.

CONFESSIONS

The scent of something savory wafted through his dreams. It was a pleasant scent, filled with memories and promises. Many of them were pleasant.

"Wakey, wakey, Kane," said a familiar voice from above.

The pleasant sensations faded with the recognition of a hard floor underneath him. His eyes fluttered and opened slowly. He saw Kalidah holding out her hand.

"Time to get up, Professor."

"It's Doctor," he replied and reached up to accept her hand. He staggered a little as he stood and found himself quickly seated on the divan in Kalidah's office. Glancing quickly around, he noted Marisol standing by the window. She gave him a tired smile of concern. How long had he been out?

"You should probably eat," the Captain said as she handed him a bowl of broth, "before I tell you the bad news."

Emilio pursed his lips, nodded, and drank down the savory broth. His body was starving. No doubt it was part of the exchange. A necessary cost, he recalled from the Academy, but not one he remembered being so drained from. He had studied the process and performed it once on a Shade, during his internship. It had been done in a clinical setting, and it was very different. This entire situation was very different.

It was called the Wrixlian Rite. The rite allowed the ritualist to stabilize a fading spirit or establish coherency in a shade. True Necromancy would have required him to spill the blood of an animal, and to draw the symbols in blood on his arm to give a shade a sense of temporary lucidity. The shade would absorb the blood from the animal and allow them to talk. The altered rite allowed for it to be done without bloodshed. Emilio preferred this option. However, a Spirit was a more complex creature than a Shade, and the rite had taken more of himself than intended. He looked over at Marisol. She appeared fine, but there was something different about her. Her aura fluctuated between blues and purples. She was in pain emotionally but trying to mask it behind the stoicism that the crown taught her. He nodded silently to himself and filed the information away.

He took another deep drink of the broth. "Go ahead."

"The Queen knows Marisol is here." Kalidah began, "It can perceive her in the same way that you allowed me to."

Emilio sputtered through his stew and shook his head, "I'm sorry, what?"

From across the room, Marisol nodded, "Whatever you put on the Captain's eyes, she … that thing … was wearing it too. You were unconscious from your endeavors and safely locked in here. I needed to see Lykos. When I arrived ...it... was there. She .. it... that thing... looked at me...she looked right at me and smiled."

Marisol gripped her hands together and looked away. Emilio considered her words and waited for a few beats, silently measuring Marisol's rage. Nothing happened. There was no tangible sense of anger or rage. His eyes moved towards her again. Swirls of deep blue flowed around her. What she had seen had clearly caused her deep pain.

Looking over to the Captain, "If the Queen is using a salve, then it means the creature is being assisted."

Kalidah scowled at the comment, "Someone has a plan in motion and it required my Queen to be murdered. The question is who and to what ends?"

Emilio slowly shook his head. "That I cannot answer. The salve I have is one that I make myself. That little container is all I have. It is not a difficult recipe, and one of the first ones we are taught at Academy." he set his bowl aside carefully. "Someone is supplying that creature, but I assure you, it is not me. However, there is some good news."

Both Kalidah and Marisol perked up. "By all means, Kane, share with the class," Kalidah said.

"Her Majesty's body is certainly here in the Hall." He said plainly. "The creature must have it secreted away in a place no one would look, but one that is easy enough to access so that it can maintain contact daily. Which is needed to refresh its disguise," he added the last part quickly. He reached up and rubbed his upper lip between his thumb and forefinger in thought, "Which also means her body is being preserved somehow. Probably magical. That means…"

Kalidah cut him off. "Ugh - more damn magic!" she glared at Emilio and demanded, "Does this mean we have a true Necromancer running around!?"

Emilio sighed. His shoulders rose and fell slightly. "Yes? No? Maybe. I don't know." he finally settled. He glanced up at Kalidah. "Anyone with a skill for magic and the proper training can employ rites or spells. Even necromantic ones, though typically with far less success than one born with the gift itself."

"How very assuring."

"I cannot change how magic works, Kalidah." Emilio offered.

"I am uncertain you would if you could."

Emilio closed his eyes and took a deep breath. "I can only apologize so many times for things beyond my control." His eyes opened and rested on the Captain. "Can we have this argument at another time, Captain? There is a small, and I mean tiny, chance that I may yet save Marisol."

Marisol's head whipped around at the comment, "What are you talking about, Emilio?"

He stood and addressed the spirit that Kalidah could not hear.

"Your body is being kept in stasis somewhere. Being prevented from the natural state of decay. Your features are unmarked. Likewise, your spirit is reflecting no signs of decomposition. If it were not for the transparency of your form, you look almost alive." He focused clearly on Marisol. "This means the creature somehow preserved you at the very moment of your death. A week has passed, but clearly, that time has not touched your shell. If we can find your body... I... might... be able to reunite you?" he said to her.

The giant figure of Kalidah stepped between the two of them, cutting in. "Alright Emilio, how can we make this miracle happen?" Kalidah asked pointedly.

For a moment, Emilio thought about it. The reply was cautious but honest.

"Only one group holds that information. The Barrow Scholars. If I ..." his words were cut short by the cold steel pressed on his bare throat. He raised his hands in defense as Kalidah forced him against the wall.

"Be very careful with your next words, Kane."

"I mean no offense, they are the only ones..."

Marisol shouted in protest, but the Captain of the Guard could not hear her orders.

"If you think I would EVER allow you to access that accursed place, you have come here in error, Doctor Kane," Kalidah said. The blade's cool metal pressed deeper against his skin.

The air suddenly chilled, and a rime of ice dusted Kalidah's sword. Emilio's eyes went wide, "No Mari.."

The windows iced over and the candles snuffed out.

"YOU WILL STAND DOWN NOW CAPTAIN!" Marisol's voice boomed.

Standing before them was a figure that resembled Queen Marisol. A woman who used to be kind. But this was not Marisol. This was a creature cloaked in the mantle of anger, wielding the power of fear. Kalidah's eyes widened in horror. Her blade clattered to the floor, and she backed away to the far corner of the room.

Emilio focused on the Queen. Sparks of red danced in her aura.

No.

"Marisol - look at me," Emilio pleaded. "Please look at me."

The Queen's glare dragged away from the cowering figure of the Captain in the corner and locked onto the Necromist. "Tell me now, Doctor Kane," she demanded. Her words burned with the power of fear and rage that was laced within them.

"When you offered to bring me here, was it out of simple goodwill?" She moved from her place across the room and approached him. The cloud of ice and chill followed in her wake. "Or did you covet the power in Barrows Hall?" Emilio felt the words hit his body like icy gusts. He needed to bring her back down or she would be lost.

Dropping his hands to his sides, palms facing outward, he addressed the angered spirit of the Queen.

"Your Majesty, when you came to me that night, we talked. Do you remember that? We talked about how much time had passed. Remember? We talked about the doppelgänger, and how it had to have preserved you?"

The angered spirit ceased its menacing approach and listened.

"I told you then that I knew you were being preserved... and I went back downstairs to my workshop to rest so we could leave the next morning. Do you remember that?"

The sparks of red that surrounded the spirit seemed to lessen. The chill in the air backed off.

"Marisol, that night in the workshop... I didn't sleep," Emilio admitted. "I stayed up researching everything I could to see if there was a way a soul could be restored to its body. I found footnotes, here and there. They all indicated that those skills died with Barrows Hall." He took a careful step forward, "I took a chance that if I could get to The Barrows ... I might learn how to get you back into your body." Another step. "I knew if I told you what I planned to do... what I planned to invoke...you might not have been willing to come this far. Please... you have to believe me. I'm just trying to help reunite you with Lykos." He held his left hand out to her.

The mention of Lykos' name broke the hold of rage on the spirit. The chill in the air dropped, and the sense of foreboding ended. The oppressive bubble of fear broke and its tension vanished. Marisol staggered and fell forward as her knees gave out from under her. The necromist stepped in quickly to catch the falling spirit and cradled her gently in his arms.

"I've got you. You are going to be fine," he whispered.

Marisol clung to Emilio as the power of the manifestation slowly faded from her, and she allowed him to guide her back to the divan.

She sat silently, Emilio beside her, cradling her hand. Then she raised her eyes to look at Kalidah.

"I'm so sorry," Marisol whispered. At that moment, the Captain heard the words of her Queen, and then the shroud of the dead fell upon her once more, leaving only silence in the room.

Some minutes passed before Kalidah moved. She knew fear, but that was something else. What shook her was something primal. It was born from the fear man had of the dark and the unknown. Wielding such power was ... unnatural, but her friend was no longer ... natural. As much as she hated to admit it, Emilio was doing everything he could to keep that primal power at bay. Worse, she needed him and his gift. Marisol needed him. Taking a deep breath, she rose from the corner and picked up the sword. Not looking at the pair on the divan, she slid the blade back into its scabbard.

"Stay here, both of you … please," she said calmly, and then walked out, locking the door behind her.

Normally a sense of fear would have driven up his anxiety, but all of that emotional turmoil was pushed aside for the woman on the divan. Holding her hand, he continued to scan her features and the surrounding light. There was no trace of the red veins running through her aura. Instead, her aura pulsed between her normal blue to that haze of purple. It almost reminded him of a heartbeat.

Even though her eyes were closed, he spoke to her softly, "Shades have to be prompted to manifest. More often than not, they fray and wither under the strain of willpower that has to be spent in doing so. Their cup is finite, so eventually, that which holds them together as a ghost simply fades away. Spirits like you … your well is as vast and deep as it was in life. Had I met you before all of this, I would have thought of you as a force to be reckoned with. In the state of being that you are now, doubly so. However, it will tax you. It will be some time before you can do that again. There are…" he paused and listened to everything around him. Confident that they were alone, he continued, "There are other things you can do. Other things you are capable of…both great and terrible. I rarely bring them up because a Spirit's time is fleeting as I help them move on. Yet, you are discovering more and more simply because of who you are. I shouldn't be surprised, but you continue to amaze me at every turn. I don't need to tell you what an amazing, kind, and courageous woman you are … I … Lykos, is fortunate to have you in his life."

At the mention of Lykos' name, he could feel her hand gently grip his. He caught himself at the last moment. He should not be saying things like that. Kalidah probably would have relieved his head from his shoulders if she caught him speaking to the Queen like this. Yet, in two days of traveling with Marisol, he found something inside himself that he'd forgotten, a spark of kinship. It was rocky and unpolished, but there was something there. Looking down at her, he slowly placed her hand to the side and stood up. He could not let that spark grow.

Walking over to the chair across from the desk, he took a seat and closed his eyes. "Whatever may come will come," he said to the air, and soon fell asleep.

TRUST GOES BOTH WAYS

Marisol was aware of everything around her. Although she could barely move, she sensed everything in the room. She could sense Emilio sleeping. He was exhausted, like her. Slowly opening her eyes, she turned her head and looked at him. The doctor had not lied outright. This much was true. He was correct; he confessed his intentions initially. She would have left him at that moment. Though she was uncertain where she would have gone.

When she manifested, she could feel the air on her skin and the warmth of the anger flushing her cheeks. She remembered the look of terror on Kalidah's face. She remembered her friend fleeing from her presence. But not this man. He stood his ground despite the threat to his life and talked to her. Helped her remember who she was. Held her. He sat with her and held her hand. He spoke to her, and she could feel the truth in his words. She could feel it in his hands, in his voice. She felt his omission. He wanted to say something else. He wanted to say *I am very fortunate to have you in my life.* The omission was the reason she gripped his hand. He was not risking his life to put a spirit at rest.

He was risking his life for her.

Kalidah returned, a tired look on her face. Over her shoulder was a large bag that sounded like a mix of muffled metal. She closed the door, locked it again, and turned to face Emilio. "Catch," she said and hefted the bag at him.

The sixty-pound bag would have knocked him off his feet if he were not already sitting down, "Oof! Gods - what is this?" he asked.

"A change of clothes, armor, and gear. Put it on." She commanded.

"What? Change here ..." he looked around.

Kalidah rolled her eyes and turned her back to him. "Honestly, Kane, for someone as familiar with the human body as you are, you are terribly uptight."

Emilio scrambled to gather the bag and moved to step behind Kalidah's desk. It offered some limited privacy.

"Yes, and I always ask permission of the dead before viewing them. It's polite." Emilio countered.

Marisol continued to watch Emilio from across the room.

He gestured at her and cleared his throat.

She smiled, inclined her head and turned to grant him his privacy to change clothes.

"Inside the bag, you will find some light leather armor, a breastplate, riding boots, and a cloak, as well as a few weapons," Kalidah said."You will also find an extra shoulder pauldron. Hand that to me when you're ready.

Emilio fumbled with the contents of the bag. "I never understood the need for armor. With the advent of gunpowder weapons, it seems so redundant..." he muttered.

"Kane, when did you see a ghost draw down on you with a rifle?"

"Point taken. Armor it is."

He rarely wore armor. He had been assigned a set at the Academy. Every recruit was. It had been years since he was forced to do it. He wasn't even certain which trunk it was in at home. He sighed in resignation, slipped his suspenders off, and began to dress.

"You will want to wait to put the gorget on, otherwise, the chest and back will not fit correctly." Marisol commented from across the room, as she watched his reflection in the glass.

He paused. He was an idiot. She was right. Shaking his head to himself, he loosened up the strap on the neck armor as directed.

Reaching into the bag, he found the spare pauldron and placed it on Kalidah's desk.

"Are you decent yet?" the Captain asked.

"My dignity is covered, Captain. Thank you." he responded.

"Is that what we are calling it?" Kalidah turned and walked back to her desk. She sat down and looked at Emilio. "You can finish elsewhere." She opened the drawers, looking for something.

Emilio scowled and then bowed in Kalidah's direction. He reached down and grabbed the bag full of armor parts and dragged it across the room back to the divan.

"Chest first, strapping the back to the front buckles. From there, your arms, biceps, elbow, forearm. You should be able to flex and have most of your range of movement. Then finally the gorget to protect your neck," she instructed.

He looked over at her as he followed her instructions.

"I used to watch Lykos put on his riding gear every morning. I know the routine by heart."

Emilio nodded in silent thanks.

"There, that should do it." Kalidah said.

Emilio and Marisol looked back at Kalidah. Both faces were filled with curiosity, but Emilio's face shifted to horror.

Kalidah had pulled several jars of paint from her desk drawers. Red, gold, black, and white. She painted the pauldron white, and in its center painted a black pentacle. An encircled star. But half of the pentacle was missing. Breaking out of the other half of the area, where the rest of the pentacle should have been, was a gold and red sun.

Emilio knew the image immediately. The sigil of the Inquisitors of Hil.

"Are you TRYING to get me murdered? Impersonating an Inquisitor! Why don't you just shoot me now!" Emilio said.

Kalidah frowned. She turned to Marisol. " Allow me to preface this with ... I do not approve of this, your Majesty." then she focused back on Emilio. "You want my help to get to the Barrows Hall? Then you are going to play by my rules." She paused and rubbed the bridge of her nose with her thumb and forefinger. "I have known you long enough to know that you will not stop until you solve this, Emilio. Extreme circumstances. Extreme measures. You have yours. I have mine." She dropped her hand from her nose and looked up at Emilio.

" I need you to trust me, Emilio, like I am trusting you now. "

The closeness Kalidah and Emilio shared as children had faded when he went to the Academy. It was inevitable. When he returned to The Reach, he did his best to avoid her altogether. When her father passed and Jessup reached out to him, he felt a sense of hope of rekindling a friendship. But she was different. Harder. Even more skeptical of what he did. He did not blame her. People don't accept the concept of magic. Many fear it because of its destructive power. Yet, the real destructive power was what it did to those you called friends. At this moment, Emilio felt it in her word and saw it on her face. She was making an effort, and he needed to do the same.

Nodding his head, he took a seat across from Kalidah. "Why an Inquisitor and not a member of the Salon?"

"The Inquisitors are the only ones who can access the Barrows alone. They send one of theirs to the Barrows every so often to ensure that the place is free of activity. The Reach has a border outpost assigned there. You will need to leave at dawn and follow the Saads Road through the woods. You must keep this sigil covered under the riding cloak at all times. When you get stopped by the outpost guards, throw your cloak over your shoulder to reveal the sigil. They'll let you through when you do this." Kalidah took out a small velvet pouch and pulled out a silvery icon. The sigil of the Inquisitors and The Reach was the same as the icon.

Marisol's eyes widen, "You did not take that from Lykos's study, did you?" she said aloud, but then sighed to Kalidah, *Steal King's Study?*

Kalidah sighed, "Yes. I did. You can report me after you're alive and well."

Marisol's eyes rolled, "My concern is for you," she said, but what was signed came out more like *Stupid - Concern for You.*

"Thank you for your concern, but that is the plan. It's the only way to get you in. From there, it's up to the both of you. Now I've packed a dual-shot pistol and a short sword. You will want to make sure both are visible when you ride. I will holster a longshot rifle in your horse's gear. You don't have to use them, but they are all necessary for the look. I've seen enough of them to know how they travel with their gear," she said.

Emilio gave a forced smile, "I usually work with a scalpel, and not this ... cleaver... but I will do my best. If there is an answer in the Barrows, I will find it," he said.

"For all our sakes, Emilio, I hope you do," Kalidah said. Her expression darkened for a moment. "If I find out that you are going there with other intentions, I will ensure you are beaten within an inch of your life, and then will gleefully hand you over to the Inquisitors."

Emilio pursed his lips, biting back a comment. He settled on, "I would expect no less."

"Good. Let's get going."

Outfitting a necromist with the uniform of an Inquisitor was one thing. Getting him out of Gran Salón without being noticed was something different. The Inquisitors of Hil had not been to Gran Salón in several months. Politics and ceremonies were involved when they visited the ruling estates in the Imperium. Hil's people loved their ceremonies.

Inquisitors traveled with an entourage of the clergy, soldiers, and scholars. It wasn't enough that the Imperator granted them a wide berth on their activities, for the sake of protecting the Realm, but they had to flaunt that fact to anyone who could see it. It was possible that there were members of that branch of the faith who were not self-absorbed zealots, intent on discovering a reason to exterminate all forms of Ars Arcane - especially the Ars Necromantia. Perhaps there was an Inquisitor who did not think of themselves as a boot and the rest of the Imperium as ants.

But if there were, Emilio had never met them.

"Quit pulling at your gorget," Kalidah said. She led a sorrel-colored pony out from the stables and over to where Emilio stood.

"It chafes," Emilio replied. Unlike a snug collar, no amount of tugging would loosen it. He dropped his hand from the neck armor.

"Were you always this delicate?" Kalidah asked. "I don't remember you always being this delicate." She handed him the reins and patted the pony on its rump.

"I'm not delicate," he objected. "I expected padding and articulation, but I should have known that Hils' people would find one more avenue of discomfort to inflict on people." he tried to stretch and found his movements restricted. "As immovable and inflexible as they are. Charming."

"I think it's rather fetching, Doctor," Marisol commented, approaching the pair.

Emilio stood upright at the Queen's words. He blamed the armor.

"You wear a uniform at the Academy, do you not?" she inquired.

"Yes." he replied. A hint of hesitation hitched his reply."Though scholars and field medics have a little use for such extensive... metal."

"It's a learning experience, Professor." Kalidah quipped with a smirk.

"Doctor."

"Whatever."

Emilio scowled at Kalidah and turned to face Marisol. It was late. Well past sunset and on toward midnight. Most of the residents of the Hall were well asleep and only a handful of guards patrolled the walls and yard. The rain from earlier left the air heavy and sweet.

"You don't have to come with me," he told her. "I do not know what Barrows Hall will be like."

"Don't be ridiculous. I've come this far, Doctor Kane." Marisol objected.

"He's right. You can stay here." Kalidah offered. She could not hear their exchange, but watching the Queen's reactions told her everything she needed to know.

Emilio looked between the two women and then focused back on Marisol. "I'm being sent into an area that is controlled by Hil's people, Majesty. I need you to understand that."

"The followers of Hil have always been supporters of the Realm. I understand their hesitation with yourself, Doctor …"

"You are not the Queen," he said. *There. It had been said.*

Marisol blinked and stepped back. "Excuse me?"

"To them." he added quickly."They won't care who you were. They will only see who you are … what you are… now."

Flickers of white flitted through Marisol's aura, evidence of shock and disbelief. The same emotions danced behind her eyes as she clearly fought to maintain the trained mask that royalty wore so often.

"My lady …" Kalidah said.

Marisol waved her off. *No.* She gestured.

"I'm sorry, Majesty, but the keepers of the place where I am going will just as surely end your existence as my own. You need to understand that."

Marisol looked between Kalidah and Emilio and then back to the Hall. A light flickered in one window in the distance. She closed her eyes and turned back to face the necromist.

"And if I remain here, the creature wearing my body may find me and end any chance of success we have."

Creature. Window. Leaving. She gestured to Kalidah.

The Captain's eyes snapped to the lighted window. She stepped between the ghostly shape of the Queen and the eyeline of anyone looking into the courtyard. Emilio's gaze followed the gesture. He adjusted the pony, using its bulk as a shield.

"I understand." he offered.

"All right." Kalidah interrupted. "It's dark, and will be for several hours." She patted the pony on the neck and looked down at Emilio. "You can ride her, but I don't recommend it until you get better light. Just walk calmly out the gates, and no one will pay you any mind. A trail that leads south is two hours down the main road. It's poorly marked, but look for three white stones about knee height. Take that trail for just shy of a mile and you will find a messenger's shack along the river. It's been out of use for a while by the troops. Can't promise its condition, but it should be empty. You can wait there until dawn. Barrows Hall will be half a day on horseback from there."

The Captain shifted to face the Spirit of the Queen. She set her jaw and straightened her shoulders, "Come back to us, My Lady. I will keep my steel sharp until you return."

"Thank you, Captain." *My thanks*, she gestured.

"Two hours out?" Kane asked.

"Two hours," Kalidah replied.

After nodding and checking the straps on the pony, he turned and extended his hand to the Captain.

"Thank you, Kal."

Kalidah reached out and clasped the outstretched arm firmly and looked into the eyes of the man she had known most of her life. "I'm not doing this for you, Kane."

"Of course not," he smiled softly, then guided them to the gates.

FOLLOW THE ROAD

A lone traveler. A simple nod from the gate guard. No questions, no comments. They exited Gran Salón with much less attention than when they entered hours earlier. It was dark, and it was quiet. The rain from earlier in the evening ended, leaving the sky above fresh and clear. The sprinkling of light from the stars across the dark canvas of the sky and the half-sliver of the moon were their only guides along the way. The only sound made at all was the slow clopping of the horse as he followed behind.

It was unnecessary that Marisol remain quiet as they journeyed. No one could hear her but Emilio. However, her silence helped to ensure he was not tempted to engage in a conversation that may be difficult to explain if they were encountered.

The armor was a foreign thing upon his body. It weighed him down and chafed as he walked. He was a physician, not a soldier. The whole ruse was irritating, despite its necessity. Traveling as a fighter was troublesome enough. Traveling as one of Hil's own chilled him to his core.

Once, in times long passed, Hil had been a deity of light and life. An inspiration and guide that spoke of creation and protection from harm. A healer. The Death Mages had changed that for everyone. The light that once stood as a gentle guide and warm welcome now focused its trained gaze on the world with baleful intent to uncover wickedness, no matter the cost.

It would not matter that Emilio was seeking to protect the realm. It would not matter that he was in the company of the Queen's murdered soul, seeking a balm for her existence. He was a magician with the ability to command the dead. It was enough. His imitation of one of their own would add to the condemnation.

You have lost your damned mind. He thought to himself as they walked along in silence. *They are going to kill you in a legendary fashion when you are discovered. You know this.*

He nodded to himself as he walked alongside the horse that Kalidah had supplied them. The saddlebags contained a bedroll and a pack of supplies. With hope, they would not be gone more than a day or two. There should be fodder at the messenger station for the horse, Kalidah assured him.

You worry about the horse and the Queen and not yourself? He argued. It was too late for arguing. It had been too late the moment he agreed to follow Marisol's suggestion about the peppered broth back at the Guild Station. He'd willingly followed the instructions of a Spirit and never once questioned what trouble it might bring him. Why?

His eyes glanced in Marisol's direction. The spirit of the Queen floated effortlessly next to him. Her proud visage was present even now. The right corner of his mouth turned up slightly as he remembered explaining to her she did not need a horse for travel. She was no longer bound by the forces of the earth. She had been put out initially, when Kalidah had not supplied her with her own mount, but was thrilled to discover she could fly.

He caught himself staring at her in the moonlight and jerked his gaze away and back to the road.

Follow the road.

They came upon the small set of white standing stones two hours into their journey, just as Kalidah said. A group of fireflies hovered around them like a collection of willow wisps. Ominous, yet promising. The trail was exactly where she said it would be. Pushing through the overgrowth, they ventured off the main road and deeper into the darkness.

The splashing sound of water soon greeted them, along with its sweet scent on the night air. They were approaching a river.

"It should be around here," Emilio whispered quietly.

Marisol nodded and floated ahead of Emilio and the horse, searching along the trail and the bank of the river for the messenger station. His chest tightened slightly when she disappeared momentarily from view and he released a held breath when he saw her wave to him from a sheltered area off the trail.

Set back from the main road, and covered by overgrowth, was a small shack, easily missed unless one was actively looking for it. It was not a large building, clearly designed to serve the singular purpose of a way station. A small stall was behind the building. It was serviceable, and that was all that mattered. Emilio took a few moments to secure the horse, search about for some dried alfalfa and fill the trough with water from the river, then managed his way inside.

The shack was just big enough to house two single beds, a few mostly empty shelves, and a cast-iron stove. It was musty and very much smelled of traveling messengers. Kalidah had thought it was abandoned. He would have to let her know when they returned.

The thatch roof needed mending in one corner, and one of the window panes was broken. Shards of glass littered the earthen floor. While not in complete disrepair, it was less than inviting. But it served its purpose. Emilio carefully shoved the shards of glass out of the way with a booted foot and gently tested one bed. Nothing scurried out, and it did not collapse. He sighed and slowly sat, letting the day's stress sink into the mattress beneath him.

Marisol glanced around the room and then sat on the other bed opposite him.

"Should I take first watch?" she asked, breaking the long silence between them.

Midway through loosening his unforgiving gorget, Emilio paused and gave a tired laugh. Marisol smiled. Given everything that had happened between them in the last few days, his laughter was welcomed.

"I will not object, but I think you might be up the full night because my body is screaming for rest. While it was uncomfortable on the floor... at least Kal's office was warm," he said as he unstrapped the side buckles to his chest piece. He groaned with the release.

"Most soldiers discover a way to prop themselves up and sleep in their armor," she smiled gently.

"I am not a soldier." he answered.

"I have noticed."

He glanced in her direction and offered a tired smile.

"You and the Captain seem ... familiar?" Marisol asked.

"Kalidah?" Emilio sighed and reached up to rub the back of his neck. "Maybe? Once? A long time ago." he offered.

"She's a good woman. I can understand the attraction."

"What? Oh! No." He sat up quickly and looked at Marisol. "Nothing like that at all. We were close ... friends... that's all...before I went to Academy." he chuckled a little."Kal's not built for romance or relationships like that." he explained. "Never has been." a note of sadness flavored his voice.

"I just miss my friend sometimes."

"I'm sorry. I ... didn't realize."

"She is a loyal member of the Imperium, and I am ... what I am." he shrugged a little, then pushed himself out of the bed to examine the stove.

"Perhaps she will see things differently when this is all done?" Marisol offered softly.

Emilio grimaced a little at the glimmer of hope offered, and the pain associated with it.

"One battle at a time." he replied and reached for the belly of the stove. Opening it, he noted the stove was empty except for a few small stones, and it had no flue pipe.

Curious, he thought.

Reaching in, he pulled out a gray crystalline rock and smiled.

"Brilliant. Heinar Crystals! That would make sense." he nodded. Placing the stone back in, he turned to his satchel and opened it to rummage around. He finally pulled out a tinder box.

Heinar Crystals were imported from outside of the Imperium. From what he knew, they were a rare and expensive commodity. Those that could afford Heiner Crystals never had to worry about cutting firewood. The crystals bore the amazing property of absorbing heat from a nearby source, storing it and releasing it over several hours. The more stones, the more hours of heat you got before you had to reignite them. Their best feature was that it was a smokeless heat so there was no need for flue pipe. It was a very handy feature if you wanted to remain unnoticed, but still keep warm. It would make sense for them to be in use if this were a hidden location. However, Emilio wondered at their expense for a shack that was supposedly abandoned.

Lighting a blackened twig he spied on the ground, Emilio held the flame to the crystal. Soon it glowed with a slight red hue that spread to the other crystals inside. The chill in the air soon gave way to a comfortable warmth.

Sitting back on the bed, he stretched out and felt his bones pop with a grateful groan, "Yes - first light, we'll feed and water the horse and then head for the checkpoint."

"Get some sleep Doctor, we have Hil's work in the morning," she said.

He forced a closed smile and nodded his head. If the last two days were long, tomorrow was going to feel like forever.

Dawn's first light came sooner than expected. He felt like he had just closed his eyes when the light hit him. His sleep had been dreamless. It was as if he knew he was unconscious but had not the energy to generate anything imaginative. Part of him was thankful for the reprieve.

He opened his eyes slowly and then draped his arm across his face to shield them from the light peering in through the window.

Marisol sat across from him. She glanced at the sunlight breaking through the window. "Welcome back Doctor, how did you sleep?"

"Honestly, not enough," he said as he stretched out into a yawn. He covered his mouth out of politeness and slowly rolled himself into a sitting position. The bed had not been too terrible to sleep upon, and thankfully without bed bugs. Reaching over to the pack Kalidah provided, he pulled out a canteen of water and took a few deep gulps. His own hunger woke up as well, and he explored inside for foodstuffs. He was rewarded with a few wrapped items tucked away: bread, dried meat, hard cheese, and an apple. Tearing off a chunk of bread, he chewed it slowly. He wanted to stuff as much as he could into his mouth, but care needed to be taken. He needed the food. His body ached for it, but not to the point of stomach cramps or nausea. A stew or soup would have been better, though he did not know how it would have been packed. His eyes glanced toward the shelves, silently hoping for a small pot and some rolled oats. There was nothing. Now was not the time to complain. At least he had something to eat.

After eating his fill, he could feel his body's other needs calling for relief. "If you will excuse me," he said and sheepishly headed outside.

Marisol watched him leave. During the few hours he allowed himself to rest, he made very little noise or sign that he was asleep. It was only the evenness of his breathing that gave it away. She watched his features and could see the telltale signs of exhaustion creeping over his face, his darkened eyes and dark stubble on his face. Lykos often bore a similar look when he had been locked in sessions with his staff, trying to sort some issue that had affected The Reach.

Emilio's exhaustion seemed different. It was not merely his body that suffered. Marisol sensed it somehow ran deeper.

She knew Emilio had undertaken a trial or ritual to preserve her after she had forcibly possessed his body. She regretted doing so. It had been a terrible violation on her part. She did not realize what it entailed at the time or the toll it would take on them both. There had been neither time nor place to discuss it since the incident. All she knew was that she had felt more... whole... after his actions.

His sacrifice.

The ability to wield magic was a rare trait in the world. Those who possessed the ability to wield it to its fullest potential were even rarer. The human body, for all its marvels, was simply not designed to channel such raw power. Those magicians who tapped into these elemental forces often found their bodies consumed by the very power they tried to wield.

Necromancy was no different in its demands. But instead of being consumed by fire and crumbling into ashes, Necromancers often became grotesque creatures of undying power who refused to die. The Death Mages of the Corpse Wars had been counted among these. While Emilio did not walk that vile path, it was clear he was paying for her existence with his own health.

Marisol surmised it was his will alone that kept him going. She could not let him sacrifice more, but she also knew that such a request would fall on deaf ears. He cared too deeply.

That much was evident, and despite her current situation, Marisol knew her own feelings were growing for him as well.

Looking down at her hand, she saw her wedding band and thought of Lykos. A man she did not choose to marry, but for whom she cared. Her husband was out of obligation and treaty.

What does until death truly mean? She wondered.

The door pushed open, and Emilio returned. He nodded to Marisol and reached for his canteen, then set it aside and began arming himself once more.

"My opinion of the Inquisitors may be biased." he began. He looked across the room to Marisol, "Is there anything to can tell me about their recent behaviors?"

"Beyond being condescending and judgemental to all those not of their faith?"

"OOO, not a fan?" he asked, tightening a strap.

Marisol pursed her lips into a scowl. "When the last Inquisitor arrived, he treated Lykos like a child, barely acknowledged my presence, and was a general prat. He made it clear that I was best seen and not heard."

"I see they have added to their levels of arrogance."

"Indeed. If you can maintain that level of self-importance and narcissism ... you will be more than convincing."

"Noted." he nodded and continued dressing.

Picking up the shoulder pauldron, he stared at the symbol Kalidah had drawn. Of all the things he despised in this world, the Inquisitors of Hil were the worst. Fastening the pauldron to his shoulder, he stood and took the riding cloak off its peg, and threw it on. Then he grabbed his pack and reached for the door.

"I like a challenge. Shall we?"

DECEPTIONS

The ride through the forest was gratefully uneventful. The rain added a chill to the morning air. Once they cleared the treeline, Emilio mounted the horse and quickened their pace. Wild fields and the occasional plume of smoke from a distant home surrounded them. A rider headed upriver passed them once, as well as a wagon filled with goods for a nearby settlement. These were the only other travelers they encountered. Fields gave way to low hills and finally slopes of mountains. They stopped after a few hours to give the horse a break and to stretch. Emilio was thankful for the rest. He was not unfamiliar with riding a horse, but riding one in armor was a very different experience. It was not one he was eager to repeat.

"Since I have done so already," she started as they rode, "Outside of possession, what else can I do in this form?"

He had been waiting for this conversation. "As I had mentioned, a Spirit's strength lies in its own will. A willful Spirit can possess a person or manifest their presence. If a Shade does so - they risk wasting whatever reserves bind them to this world. A Spirit has a well that can be refilled," Emilio said.

"Is it necessary for a spirit to be fully manifest to be heard?" she asked.

"Mmm. No. You have it backward. It takes more will and focus to manifest yourself into the world of flesh. A Spirit ... with basic focus could manifest just their voice, or enough force to move an object," he said, but turned back and shot her a warning glance, "However, too much activity can wear down your reserve. It makes you susceptible to those base emotions ... in your case, the Rage that hides within you. As your physician, I kindly ask that you refrain from such activities."

Marisol chuckled a little at his humor. She opened her mouth to comment, but something took her attention. She sensed it before Emilio. Something heavy and cold that thrummed with the slow pulse of a heartbeat. It swallowed her entire being with its presence, demanding attention. The beacon above Emilio's home had been warm and inviting. A cup of mulled cider on a cold morning. This was different. There was comfort and power here. Its lure was almost intoxicating. Death was in the distance.

"I think we are getting near The Barrows," she said.

Emilio nodded his head and glanced around. He felt the change in the power surrounding him.

"Yes, there is ... power ... here." He pulled the horse up to pause their pace as he examined the area. He took in a deep breath and closed his eyes. The horse whickered uncomfortably. Emilio nodded. "The mountain bones extend deep below." He opened his eyes and settled into the saddle.

"We are close now." he glanced to Marisol. "They may or may not have someone with the Sight in their company. It would be best if you tried to stay as hidden as you can."

The Queen's spirit nodded and floated away and into the nearby treeline, hoping to skirt the area while Emilio drew their attention.

Emilio sat up in the saddle and straightened his shoulders.

"Arrogant. Self-important. They would not dare question me ..." he said to himself, "I'm going to be dead before sunset..." he sighed and urged the horse forward.

The road that led into The Barrows ended at a fortification. The Barrows were located at the base of a mountain. Tall barrier walls extended in either direction from the great gates that barred the entrance. Impressive watch towers rose from the earth at half-mile intervals along the stretch of the barrier. Black volcanic stones surrounded the area. The entrance to The Barrows was buried deep within the extinct volcanic structure. A dedicated interloper might wander well past the expanse of the barrier walls to circumvent them, but would still have to navigate the sharp black stones. Not an easy hike for even the most skilled climber. The other challenge was having to contend with the various creatures that called the range their home. Serpents and other venomous predators dwelled here, and any attempt to traverse it was a death sentence. Whether they were native to the area, brought in by Hil's people, or drawn by the energy of The Barrows itself, was hard to determine.

There was only one entrance into the labyrinth beyond. This was the enclosure before him. Guarded and watched with zealous intent.

As Emilio approached, he noted growing activity along the allure walkway. Figures along the walls and in the towers. His keen eyes readily identified long rifles pointed in his direction.

Gunpowder. Lovely.

He glanced at his breast piece, realizing it would do precious little to stop an iron shot, even at this distance.

The massive gates slowly opened and three riders emerged from within. The look on their faces were grim and serious.

"Identify yourself, sir!" spoke the lead rider. One rider beside him rested his right hand on the butt of a wheel-lock pistol, poised to be drawn. The other rested his hand calmly on the ornate pommel of a saber.

Emilio took a breath, slightly lifted his chin, and scowled at them, "Is this how you treat the Hands of the Faithful?"

The phrase gave the lead rider pause, but he pressed on, "Very well, sir, name your Authority."

An old memory filled Emilio's mind from his time at the Academy, "I see manners are not completely foreign here. I speak with the Authority granted by those *Most* favored by Hil in all of Their Glory." Lifting his arm slowly, he threw the riding cloak off his shoulder, revealing the Inquisitor's sigil.

The revelation resulted in the surprise hesitation that Kalidah had promised. He paused and considered Emilio a moment, then looked past him, and up the trail, "Tell me, Inquisitor, where is your entourage? I find it odd you travel alone."

"I find it very odd you would question a Servant of the Cleansing Light!" Emilio snapped back, without hesitation. It was the right choice. All three men sat a little more straight in their saddles as Emilio continued.

"Do you claim to be so well versed in the procedures of those that bear the weight of vigilance for this world?" he demanded. His heart pounded in his ears as he continued. "I see no mark of the faithful on your bearing, sir." his hand drifted to rest on the end of his saber. "Should ask your name ... or perhaps the names of those you call kin?"

The rider's face twitched slightly. "I am Corporal Hatzel. Apologies. A visit from the Servants of Hil was unscheduled, sir. You come alone, bearing no obvious identification or association. You must understand our position to maintain our duty and the safety of The Barrows."

Emilio rolled his eyes and sighed. "Very well, Corporal Hatzel. I am Inquisitor Tomas Markis, Servant of the Second Light of Hil," he said as he reached into a pouch and carefully pulled out the icon given to him. Holding it up high for all to see, the icon shined brightly in the noonday light, "... and by the Authority of the Sovereignty of The Reach, I have come here at the request of King Lykos on a confidential matter concerning The Barrows."

Hatzel's eyes fixed on the sigil as the light glinted off of it. Emilio waited long enough for him to note it, then carefully tucked it away once more.

"This is a matter shared by the Servants of the Cleansing Light and called upon by your King, Lykos Eskill himself. If it were my decision, I would be elsewhere hunting those that endanger our world in their unnatural ways. Instead, I am here acting on Faith's behalf for the benefit of your King and The Reach. Does this satisfy your questions, Corporal Hatzel?" Emilio stared at Hatzel with exhausted eyes full of disdain.

Hatzel simply nodded his head. Lifting his arm, he held up two fingers. The long rifles along the wall withdrew from their bays. Inwardly, Emilio let out an internal sigh of relief.

"Apologies Inquisitor Markis," Hatzel started.

"Yes, yes... you were doing your job. Now if this quaint exercise is over, I am wasting time and daylight," Emilio said. "I do not wish to be in this ... sullied location... any longer than needed."

Emilio could see the man's jaws tighten and rather than saying anything, he pulled on the horse's reins to wheel the beast around, "OPEN THE GATES," he called out.

The huge gates to the fort opened again, and Emilio followed the riders.

Please believe me, please believe me, please believe me.

Once past the threshold, Emilio could hear the massive doors closing behind him. He could feel the weight of many eyes on him. A curt nod from Emilio here and there sent the curious on their way. A set of much smaller gates opened for him on the back side of the fort. Glancing at the walls, he noted riflemen were stationed here as well, their muzzles pointed toward the entrance of The Barrows.

Designed to keep things inside The Barrows, he noted.

If any stationed here bore the Sight, it would be these.

His eyes searched the area quickly, seeking sigils or other signs of Necromantia. There were none.

Idiots. This is where you want your wards. Emilio swore silently. For a group dedicated to protecting the realm from the dangers contained within, they lacked even the most basic of protections. He knew now that there was no danger of Marisol being seen, and hoped that she would discover that on her own shortly. Hatzel and company did not proceed past the second set of doors but stepped to the side to allow Emilio to pass.

The small gates closed behind him, and he continued onward. The soldiers who stood watch gave Emilio a final passing glance before focusing their attention once more on the road ahead.

The road before him dropped into a valley of crags and broken rock. A figure stood along the side of the road ahead. It was Marisol. Her presence confirmed there was nothing to prevent the dead from entering the area. A lapse in security he would share with Kalidah when he returned. How she came upon the information would be for her to explain.

"Majesty" Emilio inclined his head politely as he approached. "You are unharmed?"

Marisol looked up at Emilio and nodded. "Not so much as a pause as I passed by them all." She turned and floated by his side as they continued.

"Concerning," he commented.

"Mmm," she agreed.

"But ... also ... comforting," Emilio said gently as he looked over at her.

She offered him a small smile in response.

As they rode forward, they noticed a single post in the ground with an iron ring fastened to it. The sigil of Hil was burned into the wood. Looking at the downward slope, they understood its meaning. They would have to travel on foot from this point forward. The rocky ground and loose stone would be the demise of any large mount. Sliding off the horse, Emilio took the pack with the gear and slung it over his shoulder. Tying the horse to the post, he patted its neck, and they carefully made their way forward.

The road before them precariously descended deeper into the valley of black and ashen stone. Their path split into multiple trails, each covered with a light blanket of gray mist that moved along the ground. To anyone else, the image was forbidding and unwelcoming. The deeper they descended into the valley, the wind picked up and pushed steam across the ground. The air was warm with a faint scent of rotten eggs. No living thing lingered in the labyrinth. Those who did not know these trails would be easily lost in the unmarked pathways. At best, one may retrace their footsteps to regain their bearings. At worst, a wrong turn could mean a fall down a deep chasm into the depths below.

For Emilio and Marisol, the path was quite clear and was, in fact, marked. Unseen by normal eyes, a glyph pulsed in stones to their left. Necromantic power stretched out like veins in stone, pointing the way.

"Here we go, Your Majesty," Emilio said with a bit of nervousness.

"Indeed, Doctor, time to tread lightly," she breathed.

INTO THE LABYRINTH

The path was meant to discourage travelers. It was very effective in its design, especially for someone in armor. The rocks underfoot were loose and made from the sharpened edges of volcanic activity centuries old. Some areas of the cave were smooth, and others felt like spikey bits of stone dripping from the ceiling. The limited light made the trek more hazardous. More than once, Emilio righted himself against the wall, narrowly avoiding a rolled ankle. There would be no extraction for him if he came to injury here. His name would be added to other scholars who dared these caves. The further they traversed, the surrounding stone seemed to curve and extend upwards as they descended the slowly enclosing pathway. What was room for two people became narrower and narrower, forcing Emilio to walk at an angle.

The faint foulness of the air from earlier faded into something earthy. Clean and dry. The dark stone walls gave the illusion of stretching above them like fingertips touching to form an archway. Tiny skylights in the broken terrain above that lent light to the underground soon ended and the bright light of day disappeared from overhead altogether. As if in trade, the path beneath his feet felt smoother and easier to traverse.

Along the walls, pale veins of stone appeared. They stretched up from the ground and reached toward the roof of the tunnel, like some strange woven lattice. They glowed slightly in the darkness. Emilio allowed these faintly glowing veins to guide his footsteps. A reasonable person would have brought a torch. Kalidah was a reasonable person and had included one in the possessions she packed for them, but something told Emilio that lighting it would be a bad idea. He was uncertain if it was science or intuition that spoke to him as he walked in the limited light of The Barrows, but he felt that anyone bearing fire or light would not be welcome here. Light was a celebrated aspect of Hil and Hil's influence was a bane upon this place.

"Is that light up ahead?" Marisol asked.

Emilio opened his eyes wider, hoping he could see more in the surrounding darkness. There was a faint green glow in the distance.

Curious.

For a moment, he looked back. The light of day was reduced to a memory after they had been walking for almost a half hour.

"With any luck, I can find the person we need and leave this place behind," he said. The darkness seemed to swallow his words.

"I thought that you of all people would be eager to explore," she remarked.

"There is an adage about cats and curiosity, Majesty," Emilio cautioned. He could not deny that part of him begged to be allowed to explore the depths of The Barrows to their fullest. It was hard to resist the wealth of information that was here. But he dare not get caught in The Barrows after the sun above had set. The dangers were immeasurable. What good would success be if they could not leave?

He needed to focus on finding a Scholar.

"Believe me, I am curious," he said as he placed a cautious hand on the wall next to him. There was a hint of ... something... at his touch. A pulse? A heartbeat? A moment of recognition? He frowned. "But we know the Inquisitors have had control over this place for decades. Gods know what they have done to it. Anything of academic value has probably been destroyed in their zealousness." He peered up at the ceiling. "I'm just hoping I might find someone who escaped their purge," he said. All of this was a gamble, but it was a gamble he had to take.

The surviving Scholars had been promised the Barrows in repayment for their efforts in ending the Corpse Wars. The Death Mages had been using the Barrows as a base of operations. While its location seemed far off the coast, the vast networks of natural tunnels and caverns were spread out underneath the Reach. Using the tireless dead, the Death Mages commanded their legions to mine and burrow along the ancient lava tubes that spread out in all directions. With these deathly tendrils, they were able to expand out of the Reach and into the continent beyond. When the Necromancers made their first moves, their forces seemed to strike out of nowhere. Coming out of the ground in droves, the dead and undead monstrosities ravaged the countryside. Towns and villages full of life soon became ghost towns as hordes dragged both the dead and living into the dark earth below. From there, it was surmised that those taken into the Barrows would become unwilling participants of both foul and profane necromantic rites. Those victims would serve in the ever-growing legions of the undead. Their purpose there was simple; to cleanse the earth of its infecting darkness, and strike out the evil that had taken root in its halls.

If it were not for the Scholars who stood against those abominations, the Death Mages' dream of domination would have come true. It took those who understood the magic involved to turn it against them and, with it, the tide of the war. When the war ended, the Scholars were led by their victorious allies, the Light of Hil, a Calvary of Light Mages and Warriors into The Barrows.

It was there, under the orders of the Imperator, that the Light of Hil turned on those who had granted them victory and slew the Scholars in their new home.

The green hue had grown bright enough that Emilio could see plainly. Looking back, the light of day was no more, not even a pinprick of memory. The narrow walls of the path had rapidly expanded so that he and Marisol stood side by side at the mouth of a larger cavern. There was a noticeable difference in the temperature. One might expect warmer temperatures, as one went deeper into old lava tubes. This was not the case here. Coolness in the air and an unnatural chill that would drive normal people away settled in upon Emilio. Despite this, there was an intense feeling of both belonging and comfort as both stood in the large cavern.

The slick volcanic rock gave way to more worked stone intermixed with gray granite. Marisol stopped and looked up. Emilio paused and followed her eye line. An archway stood before them, carved into the stone. It was clearly worked by hand; this was no natural occurrence. Strange glyphs had once been carved into the surface of the stone. Glyphs that appeared magical in design. These glyphs had been marred and destroyed by the marks of hammer and chisel, changing them and transforming the original carvings into the sigil of Hil. Untrained eyes would see only these, but to Emilio and Marisol, something deeper shone past the destruction of Hil's hand. The original power of the glyphs remained woven into the stone itself. The power of the glyphs shone in the stone.

In unison, they spoke aloud, "Life is but a Test, in Death Lies the Answers."

Marisol raised an eyebrow. "Given the state of things, I must wonder if there was an answer found."

Emilio glanced over at her, "The journey that Life takes us on always will lead to Death. While some may think it morbid, it is what it is. Those experiences shape and refine us so we can meet that next threshold of existence. Where our soul goes next is the question that fueled the Scholars and their work. Hopefully, we can find one who can tell us that and more."

"Agreed, Doctor." Marisol nodded, and before Emilio could say more, she stepped across the threshold.

A wave of power washed over them both as she breached the entranceway to the cavern beyond. Emilio gasped as he caught his breath. The sensation was intense and yet somehow also familiar. He looked over at Marisol.

The spirit of the Queen was bent forward, hands upon her knees. "Doctor, what was that?"

Emilio took a deep breath and stood up straight. "There is something, some sort of enchantment over this place."

To those without the Sight, this place would have been black as pitch. But for Emilio and the dead, the walls all around them pulsed softly with the bluish-green hint of entropic energy. These energies allowed him to see clearly, almost as though it were broad daylight. The place seemed almost alive if such a thing could be said of the energy of decline.

As he stood there marveling at the strange beauty of the cavern, a hard realization hit him. This was more than just a dark lair or base of operations. This was not only a place of wonder but a true place of power. This was why the Death Mages claimed this place as their own, and why Hil's people wanted it destroyed. This was an Entropic Nexus. A singular place where a Necromancer could pull energies from Entropy itself. The pull of such power could be endless and intoxicating, affording a magician the ability to fuel their gifts unimpeded by the need to manage resources.

Emilio closed his eyes and took a breath, centering himself. It would be so easy to lose yourself here; so easy to lose your connections with the living world. He opened his eyes once more and focused on the trappings of the area. There was something else here, something foreboding.

The hall before them felt endless. Massive carved columns rose from the base of the cavern, four or five stories high, each the width of a single house. Carved into these were sigils of power, ancient and timeless. The cavern expanded outward, all around them for what seemed like forever. Where there were walls, he could see alcoves symmetrically carved into the stone's surface. To his left, he could see several tunnels with no discernible markings. Yet one of them felt 'colder' than the rest. He could feel a chill coming from the tunnel. Tearing his attention away, he stared at the grand hall. It was impossible to determine how far the hall stretched, but it was far larger than either of them could have conceived. To say the energies here were ancient would be an understatement. It was possible that this hall was far older than the first Imperator's reign. Two hundred-plus years seemed like a flicker of a candle compared to the residual energies surrounding them.

"It's... it is as if those columns are supporting the very weight of the mountains themselves," Marisol whispered in awe as she stared upward.

Narrowing his eyes upwards, the carvings seemed familiar. "From the looks of them...these are histories, stories..." Emilio said as he tried to read the carvings. "It's the story of The Three," he said, pointing at the first column, "When the universe was created ... our world was birthed." He pointed to another section of carving and continued, "It was Hil's light that brought warmth to this world. That warmth awakened Geekind, the Hand of Nature. Geekind gave form to living things with Hil's aid."

He shifted and moved to follow the text of the carving, marveling at the discovery, then paused. There was a passage here that he knew, but one that was often translated differently. He placed his hand gently on the column and read,

"When the world became too full of living things, Styx rose from shadows and gave the gift of Death to the living so that life could be born anew. From Death there was Life."

"That's not how it goes." Marisol corrected him.

Emilio gestured at the carving, "I beg to differ ..."

"Let me see ..." Marisol said and moved closer. Her foot caught suddenly on a stone, tripping her. She fell forward.

Instinctively, Emilio rushed forward and caught Marisol in his arms. Something he should not have been able to do. Just as she should not have tripped over a stone. He felt the weight of her form fall into his arms.

Marisol stared at Emilio in surprise, then quickly righted herself, pushing out of his grasp. Wordlessly, Marisol reached out and placed her hand on Emilio's chest.

"I ... I can feel you?!" she said in wonderment.

Emilio stared down at Marisol's hand on his chest. It was solid and no longer transparent. He carefully reached forward and touched her forearm. She was, in fact, solid.

"How?" he said, but stopped. "Let us not get ahead of ourselves," He cautioned. Sliding his pack forward, he reached inside and pulled out his medical bag. Rummaging through its contents, he withdrew the purple-lensed monocle and examined the room.

All around him, he saw a necromantic power pulse, but there was something else here, too. A foreign red pulse of energy webbed itself around the cavern. He scowled.

Marisol slowly reached out and took his hand in hers. "Your hand feels warm. I... I can feel the warmth of your hand, Doctor. I can feel the coolness in the air." She took a deep breath and held his hand against her chest, but frowned slightly. He was warm, but she could not feel the beat of her heart against his hand. It was not real. She was not alive. "I can feel more... but it isn't the same. It's close to what I remember, but it feels off. What is this?"

"There is ... an enchantment... some form of a permanency rite in place. It is like the Ag Baint... the Touching spell.. but this is more lasting," he commented, referring to the spell he had used to carry her form to Kalidah's offices. He dragged his hand away from Marisol's chest and offered her a small, if pained, smile. Then he directed his gaze to the ground, looking for something.

"The Ag Baint Rite allows a Necromist to physically interact with the dead. However, it is a double-edged sword. If you can touch the dead, they can touch you, mostly. Under that ritual, if a Spirit or a Shade were to strike me, I would probably feel the hit. It might feel like a shove, but they would continue to pass through me and not cause any lasting damage. The extent of the contact is limited. This...whatever this is... is different."

"Different how?" she asked.

Emilio considered for a moment. "It could be the location itself, or it could be the alterations to the spell ... but there is more 'gravity' to it? That is the best way I could put it. Someone altered the enchantment to the point of fully physical interaction.”

Marisol opened her hand and quickly slapped him. Contact to contact, the normal resistance of flesh hitting flesh, much to the shock and surprise of them both.

"Ow! Really Marisol?!"

Marisol grinned sheepishly, "I'm sorry, I had to try -"

Emilio chuckled as he rubbed his cheek, "Well, you could have given me a bit of ..."

He stopped short as a howl echoed throughout the cavern. An unsettling and unearthly sound bounced off the walls of the cavern and seemed to come from all around them.

“What was that?” Marisol asked.

“Nothing pleasant,” said Emilio. “I don’t think we are alone.”

SACRIFICE

Signs of movement. Shadows shifting in the already murky darkness. It sounded like the clatter of bones across a rocky surface. Multiple figures darted from column to column. Emilio and Marisol could not focus on what was coming. It seemed all around them, and it was coming fast.

From behind them, there was a grating sound of stone. Turning around, Emilio saw a skeletal figure emerge from a darkened alcove.

Skeletons?

The appearance of the mobile dead spurred a thought in the Necromist. Someone had placed an enchantment here to allow the dead to interact fully with the living.

"This is a trap!" he exclaimed.

Marisol whirled around at the sound of something behind her. Gray-white flesh stretched over what remained of a skeletal frame, along with age-tattered clothing, met her gaze. It dragged itself forward and reached out a clawed hand toward her. For a moment, the gesture appeared as if it were asking for help, but the creature's face said otherwise.

A mask of unfathomable hate. Tiny red orbs of energy glowed in empty eye sockets and seemed to focus on her and Emilio.

"Ideas Doctor?" She asked and took a step closer to him.

Drawing the sword on his belt, "Get ready to run…"

Marisol considered and then reached across his chest and pulled the holstered pistol there from its rest. She cocked the hammer back, aimed, and fired at the creature. The shot rang in both their ears, echoing off of the cavern walls. Her aim was precise. The shot blew the creature's skull inward and the red light ceased as it fell to the ground.

"Or we stand our ground, Doctor," and she readied the pistol again.

Emilio blinked and stared at her in both awe and admiration.

"My Lady …"

"Compliments later, combat now, Doctor!" Marisol commented, and turned to face the oncoming horde once more.

Emilio was not a swordsman, but he knew how to defend himself. Saber and pistol were standard combat tools taught at the Academy. They were required to study, if only to understand how to defend themselves without the command of magic. He studied as was required, but he was never very good.

The first shot had been deafening and almost distracted him from the galloping figure rushing toward them. It was hard to discern whether the thing was cloaked in fabric or pure shadow. His gaze followed it as it leaped toward him.

Muscle memory from his Academy training took over.

Immediately, his arms brought the blade up into a defensive stance, and he parried the slashing strikes from the shadowed creature. He was not built for the offensive, but the defensive lessons all kicked in at once as he continued to block the creature's sharpened strikes, waiting for his moment. Finally, the creature reared back, causing another muscle memory to activate. His body shifted forward, his right arm bringing the sword down across the creature's body. He felt resistance to the momentum of the blade. It bit in but did not slice through. Instead, Emilio's blow slammed the creature to the ground. The creature turned its head upwards in an unsettling fashion and hissed at the Necromist. Rather than wait for the creature to right itself, Emilio pulled back and kicked it in the head. Something gave way from the force of the kick. The head was flung away, rolling and hissing into the darkness.

Three more deathly creatures emerged from various alcoves. They were slow, but their intent was clearly determined. Behind him, Marisol took careful aim as the new creature's speed afforded the luxury of granting better aim. Beyond them, additional shadows shifted in the distance, and flickers of red lights appeared.

Drawing his sword out of the creature's body, Emilio looked up and around, attempting to gauge the strength of the enemy. There were so many. He glanced back at Marisol and watched as she emptied the firearm into the growing assembly of red eyes.

At that moment, the pistol sounded off its final click, announcing that it was empty.

"Doctor, please tell me there is more ammunition in that bag?"

He knew there was not.

"Run for that smaller tunnel!" he shouted. He took another heavy swing of the sword. These creatures bore no flesh. At most, he was hacking at the bone. He would have had better luck with his walking stick.

Marisol did not hesitate at Emilio's command and forced herself to sprint for the smaller tunnel. Halfway to her goal, she felt a sensation which she had all but forgotten. She felt 'tired'. Gravity and exhaustion pulled at her, slowing her forward momentum.

Perplexed and panicked, she searched around for an answer.

She was only a few yards away from the mouth of the tunnel. She could feel the promise of entropic energy emanating from it, welcoming her, drawing her in. Her steps faltered, like a boot stuck in heavy mud. Looking down, she saw light red webbing reaching up and ensnaring her feet.

Another old sensation ran through her body.

Pain.

"Doctor! Emilio!" she screamed.

The cave was alive with movement. Dozens upon dozens of unliving creatures hastened toward them.

Her scream pulled his attention from the onslaught. Yards from the promise of escape. Yet, even if they made it into the tunnels, nothing was stopping these hordes from following. He watched her fall forward, catching herself on her hands. Pleading eyes looking up at him.

"Help me,"

The revenant horde of ghastly skeletal creatures seemed unending. There was only one course of action.

"Marisol, cover your ears!" he shouted as he slung the pack in front of him. He grunted at the exertion. This would have been so much easier without the encumbrance of armor.

Scrambling quickly, he fished out his medical bag and plunged his hand inside. Pulling out a small object wrapped in cloth, Emilio closed his eyes and chanted as he unwrapped the item.

The small silver bell from the Fives' station.

Soft light glinted off of its silvery surface. With every word from Emilio, the glint became a glow and then a light. Opening his eyes, Emilio watched as the horde charged at him.

"My apologies Styx," he whispered and rapidly tapped the service bell in his hand.

The chime of silver on silver rang with a clean and crisp note.

The rapid tapping of its surface was a familiar sound that many shopkeepers deaded as it meant an upset, angry, or rude customer was on the other end. In the hands of a Necromist, the silver bell was a powerful last resort. Whether it was the purity of the silver metal, which had been a gift to humanity from Geekind, or its hallowed presence in the light of Hil, was unknown. The silver bell's chimes sent shockwaves of power at the oncoming horde, blowing them back as if hit by the winds of a hurricane. The power of each blast forced the creatures back into the darkness once more.

The ancient eldritch power that surrounded them flickered with every chime. Such was the power of the simple talisman. The surge of bodies that had been pouring toward them reversed their course as they tried to escape, or collapsed into dust and ash.

Soon they were alone once more.

Emilio watched with his hand poised over the bell as the cacophony of hissing receded. His heart pounded in his ears. His mouth was dry from chanting and anxiety.

The Rite of Purga was a raw expulsion of power. It was crude and without the delicate subtlety of the Ars Necromantia. It was a rite created by the Inquisitors of Hil. The Academy provided instruction and instilled empathy in its students so they could not only navigate but understand the plight of the restless dead. However, the Inquisitors made sure that their 'philosophies' were integrated into all teachings. To them, a sympathetic hug was far less effective compared to the power of Hil's Cleansing Light. If you were born with the gift of Sight, it was the price one had to pay for their freedom.

Hil's Most Faithful did not see shades and spirits as lost souls who needed aid to find their final rest. No. The undying were those who were unworthy of Hil's final blessing. The Divine Light of Life only blessed the faithful, and so those that remained were considered abominations that needed to be driven back to the darkness where they belonged.

The Rite was effective. It drove away the dead, but it did not make them amicable toward the living in doing so. Those tortured souls who would eventually return to the location were made mad by the magic of it all. This allowed the Inquisitors the necessary justification to dispatch the restless dead in their preferred fashion, holy fire.

He hated using the bell, but there had been no other choice.

Confident that they were out of danger, Emilio turned back to Marisol. He expected to see her picking herself off the ground. Instead, a red viscous webbing bound her to the stones. It pulsed with power.

"Marisol!"

He rushed to her side and reached out to pull her from the webbing's grasp. A jolt of pain coursed through his fingers and up his arm. Like the sting of an enormous scorpion. He pulled his hand back quickly. A red trail walked up his hand and wrist.

He was not dead. This should not affect him like this.

He took a breath and reached for her once more. The stinging of a hundred jellyfish riddled his arms and hands. He gritted his teeth and clenched his jaw, forcing the helpless figure of Marisol onto her back so he could see her.

Terror-filled eyes stared up at him. Red webbing all but covered her face. Her pain-filled screams became muffled as the red webbing glowed and thickened around her body.

"Where is this coming from?!"

He quickly scanned the area, trying to find its source.

A tendril of red snapped up and tried to wrap around his wrist. He gestured at it and hissed something in an ancient tongue. Then stepped away quickly.

Where?

Marisol's screams grew quieter as the webbing thickened around her.

"NO!" he yelled and stepped toward her. Red tendrils snaked at him once more.

"Hil's Light, grant me sight!" Emilio intoned the words of Vista, invoking the power of Hil to allow him to see the source of magic. He dreaded the invocation of Hil's name in a place of entropy such as this, but there was no other way.

Forgive me.

Uncovering his eyes, he scanned the area again and saw what he dreaded.

To trap various entities, a magician could draw down a circle to imprison an elemental being or other magical creature. Such a temporary prison permitted the magician time to question the entity or perhaps to discover a means to return it back to where it belonged. They were useful tools in the arsenal of any who trafficked in magic.

The circle before him was not a typical binding circle. Whoever had created this 'ghost trap' had done so with the express purpose of not only binding a creature to one place but magically tearing the creature's essence apart. For beings such as Marisol who were self-aware, this was a horrifying experience. Emilio's stomach knotted at the realization of what was happening to her. He glanced quickly around the room, and his blood chilled. This was not the only trap. A barrier of traps had been erected around the room, one adjacent to the next. A veritable minefield of agony and destruction.

"Those goddamn monsters," he hissed.

He could still hear Marisol's muffled screams as the red cocoon continued to build. To free her, he would have to unweave the magic that bound her. But could he?

I have to try.

Careful to stay out of the reach of the tendrils, Emilio walked around the edge of the binding circle, reading the glyphs and runes there. He had not been entirely honest with Marisol in describing his knowledge of the Ars Necromantia. Emilio had spent months sitting with the spirits that were bound to the Academy, learning their stories and listening to their tales. In granting kindness and compassion to ancient spirits, he had been led to a small cache of books. Books that would earn him a painful execution at the hands of Hil's Most Faithful, if they were ever discovered.

Knowledge is not dangerous. What you do with it may be.

It was this forbidden knowledge that allowed him to re-write the beacon that hung above his home. That knowledge helped him discover less gruesome means of enacting ritae and rituals to commune with the dead.

And now that same knowledge might aid in saving Marisol.

His Queen.

His Lady.

He had to act now if he were to unweave what was put into place. Emilio read the glyphs and how they were balanced against one another. Every binding circle had to have a way to release it. Stories and legends of circles being foiled by an apprentice accidentally sweeping away a chalk mark existed for a reason. He silently wished for a mallet and chisel to destroy the ground the spell was carved into. It might have worked.

After seeing the circle in full, Emilio pieced together its structure. Once more, a chill ran through his veins. The Theurgy of Hil, as well as the trappings of older Necromantic symbolism, were spread all along it. The Inquisitors had 'warped' their Theurgy to replace necromantic bindings of power. It was hard to tell where Necromancy ended and where Theurgy began.

What have you done?

The analytical part of Emilio's brain kicked into overdrive, then he suddenly realized Marisol's pained cries had ceased.

A jolt of panic punched him in the chest as he turned once more to look at Marisol's imprisoned figure. The pulsing red of the webbing was fading. There was no longer time to solve the puzzle. Immediate action was required. If this circle was created with the foundations of Necromancy, there was one action that guaranteed power and control.

"Please be right," he pleaded and unsheathed the knife on his belt.

Gritting his teeth at the pain, he carefully sliced a sigil into the palm of his left hand. The necromantic glyph for 'Sacrifice'.

Chanting softly, he could feel the sickly green pulse of entropic energy run through him and out his arm. The mixture of his blood and the energy changed its crimson hue to a black color almost as dark as night. The blackened blood trailed down his arm and dripped upon the stones. Falling to his knees, he placed the bloody hand over Marisol's face.

"Please."

The webbing wiped away like old cobwebs as he slowly slumped across her cocooned form.

The sound of the bell had been deafening. She felt it at the core of her being. If she had been corporeal, she would have said that she felt it in her bones. Deep, sharp, incapacitating. It was more intense than anything she had ever felt in the waking world. Then a burning sensation dug into her. It was warm at first, like a hot bath, then it became blistering heat that wrapped around her and pulled her down. She remembered Emilio moving her. She remembered looking up into his eyes, pleading for help. Eyes that begged to aid her, and asked her to hold on to hope.

She tried to scream and felt hot wetness cover her face and mouth. She had no lungs, but she could not breathe. She had no skin, but she could feel it burn. There was nothing but pain. Pain and the red haze of being pulled in a hundred directions at once.

A pulse shot through her body, through the heat and the pain. A pulse of energy. It pushed at her. A thousand tiny hands trying to help her stand. But the webbing held her fast.

Another pulse. Another push.

Something brushed across her face.

Webbing broke free from across her face and she felt the chill dampness of the cavern. She had no need of air, but she gasped and gulped in desperation. Arms, once pinned to her sides, cracked their bindings, freeing her. She reached for her face and throat and pulled the webbing away, like so many rotten vines.

There was pressure on her. She shifted, forcing herself upright. The weight and pressure faded. Her eyes opened, and she stared in horror at the black ichor she was covered in. Black ichor covered the collapsed form of Emilio at her side. His left hand pulsed with the same unearthly green power as the rest of The Barrows. A strange wet sigil glowed in his palm. Black wetness, like the ichor they were both covered in.

It's not ichor. It's blood. Emilio's blood.

Marisol forced herself up and moved to Emilio's side. He looked tired...and pale. His breathing was shallow. His eyes fluttered open, and he forced a smile.

"What have you done, you foolish, foolish man?" she asked as panic seeped in.

"Saved... saving...you." He breathed.

Marisol reached for him and placed her hands on his damp flesh. The magic of The Barrows still held her shape and gave it form.

"What can I do for you?" she asked, cupping his cheek and staring down into his eyes. She could feel the sweat on his skin and the beat of his heart. It was slowing.

"Not you," he said with a long, slow blink. "Apologies. I need to borrow from this place...please..."

She opened her mouth to reply and realized he was not looking at her. He was staring off into the distance. Something in the darkness held his attention. She followed his gaze. Hordes of eyes stared back at them from the darkness. Waiting. Watching.

He was asking them for permission?

The creatures did not advance this time. Instead, many bowed their heads and backed away in deference, assuming their places of guardianship once more. Within that shuffle of sound, she heard a hiss of words.

Be Welcome.

"It's fine," he mumbled to Marisol and lightly gripped her hand with his unbloodied hand. "For the ... preservation... of... life."

His eyes closed slowly, and he murmured slightly. He splayed the fingers of his bloodied hand on the ground.

She watched the green glow pulse from his hand. That pulse was soon mimicked by the surrounding ground. Veins of entropic energy ran jaggedly, like lightning through the cavern and converged on them both. Marisol felt power run through her body. It was a mixture of pins and needles along her skin, as shocking as a dip in a cold pond. She gasped. Beside her, Emilio's body arched in unison. It was barely a moment, but they felt suspended there for what seemed like an eternity.

Then the pulsing stopped. Silence surrounded them once more.

Emilio's eyes flew open. He sat up abruptly and took in several deep breaths.

"That … was an … experience." He patted his body, as if making an assessment of himself. He focused on the carved glyph in the middle of his hand for a moment, then reached up and tore at his sleeve to fashion a crude bandage.

"Doctor, what in the gods' names did you do? What was that webbing?" Marisol asked. The experience had done something to her. She remembered exhaustion and pain. Now she felt refreshed and whole.

Emilio nodded and continued to wrap his hand.

"Hil's Most Faithful placed binding traps all along these tunnels." he began. " They destroy the undying. Ghost, ghast, revenant, everything. I think it's meant to keep them from leaving through these pathways. To prevent another army from being amassed here." He secured the bandage.

"Those creatures tear apart anything living that comes into The Barrows. If their spirit lingers the traps take care of the rest. But they couldn't nullify the power of The Barrows itself. So afterward this place resurrects the bodied and adds it to protectors."

"So all of those … creatures…"

"Were living people who came into The Barrows and made it this far. Yes."

Marisol frowned at the thought of how many people had been killed in such a fashion over the years. It was effective, but horrific.

"They said we are welcome here. Why do I feel like... I don't know how to describe it. Like I feel better than I did when we first met," she asked as she slowly stood up.

He turned toward her to answer her question.

Marisol gasped.

Emilio turned quickly to see what might have elicited such a response from her. There was nothing. He turned slowly back to Marisol. He raised his hands as if to ask a question when she gingerly reached out and touched his face.

"Your eyes Emilio... green... they are bright green. And your hair," she said as she reached out to touch it, "The entire left half of your head has gone white. Not just a lock. What is all this?"

Her hand felt soft against his cheek. Chill fingertips against his warm skin. He leaned into her touch ever so slightly. The blackened blood of his actions had already dried and flaked off her face like ash, revealing her beauty once again. He yearned to return that touch. To cradle her face in his hands and gaze into her eyes.

They stood there for a moment. Each with the other. Heartbeats alone separated them. That moment of connection between one soul and another. He felt the warmth on his face grow. Her head slightly tilted forward. The flash of her wedding band caught his eye. He blinked, breaking the connection before it could be committed.

He took a step back and instead looked at the ground.

He couldn't do this.

He sniffed and cleared his throat and stared at the ground, refusing to look up at her. "The Barrows are an Entropic Nexus. Entropy is a constant here. It is believed that a true Necromancer can drain the life force of another to fuel their own."

"Like a Vampyre?" Marisol asked quietly. She had felt the warmth on his face when he looked at her. She knew that warmth. She remembered what it felt like long ago. Before politics and arranged marriages.

"Hrmm. No. Nothing so visceral." he answered. "The entropic energy created from death might extend a life ... but it was that same practice that corrupted them. They thought they could live forever."

She watched him, standing across from her, not looking at her. Staring at the ground to focus on anything else. She knew he felt it, too. Perhaps it was the stress of the situation or the anxiety of the ordeal.

Or something else.

"Could they?"

He shrugged and nudged a stone with his toe. "Forever is a long time, my lady."

My Lady.

Two words uttered in the darkness of an ancient tomb that carried the weight of unspoken confessions.

"I asked to borrow some of the power from the nexus. The protectors allowed it ... though I'm not sure why," he said, finally looking up at her.

Confessions were written on his face and carried in his eyes. Confessions that words could never speak aloud.

It was a bittersweet pain. He was trying to do right by her. She had a husband who loved her, and she cared for him. This stranger, a man she had not known until a few days ago, was risking his life for her. He asked not for a reward, recommendation, or station. He was doing all of this to help her, knowing in the end, should they succeed, she would return to her place at Lykos' side, and none of this could ever be.

They had come here to return her to her body. To her position. To Lykos. But was that what she really wanted?

Marisol took another breath and gave him a light smile. "Maybe you gained their respect by saving one of their own."

Emilio looked at her quizzically for a moment and then looked back at the shadows. A few red lights in the darkness continued to watch. But it was no longer a gaze filled with hate. They gazed now with open curiosity at the actions of the necromist and this lady spirit.

Emilio suddenly felt embarrassed and ran his hands through his hair out of a nervous habit.

"Perhaps." he nodded. "We should probably head for that smaller tunnel," he said, turning his attention back to her. "With the trap disarmed, we should be able to pass freely."

"Of course." She gave a simple nod in reply.

THE PRICE

The tunnel was wide enough for three people to stand shoulder to shoulder and was elegantly carved. There was no iconography here, just a flowing artful design. Someone with talent had taken the time and effort to give this place a sense of 'being'. Although it was short, the tunnel left both travelers with a sense of admiration. In front of them, the light seemed to brighten, as if there was a source somewhere overhead.

Stepping out of the tunnel, they entered another large cavern. Dozens of pools of water filled the open area. Some seemed to hiss and bubble with steam while others remained as still as glass. In the far side of the cavern, a lone figure stood tending to one pool, a long staff in hand. No other occupants appeared within sight. No movement from the shadows. No glowing red eyes from hidden alcoves. The scene appeared at peace.

Sharing hesitant glances, Marisol and Emilio nodded and reached for each other's hands. The magic of The Barrows still held her form, as solid as though she were living. Emilio looked down at her hand In his. It was small and delicate, and cool to the touch. The only sign that she was other than what she appeared at this moment. He smiled softly. Nodding his head, he gave her hand a gentle squeeze, then they made their way forward.

There was a sense of sanctity here. The silence that one experienced in temples of true faith. The Imperium was filled with places of worship to the Tryad, but few carried a divine spark of power within their walls. Most were simply places dedicated to the Faith, where people gathered and mouthed memorized prayers out of duty and service. Emilio had stood in many such empty halls of worship in his days, silently hoping to feel something more.

For those who knew without failing that this physical existence was merely a pause in the soul's journey, the false trappings of faith were often raw wounds laid bare. Such was the weight of knowing that death was only part of the recipe of life.

Standing here in this place of ancient mystery, Emilio felt something he had only glimpsed once or twice in the past. A true sense of the Divine. The still quiet here was neither awkward nor foreboding. It was the gentle welcome of rest at the end of a day's hard toil. It was the warmth of a hearthstone on a fall evening that invites one to sit by the fire. It was the soft cushion of a favorite chair as one settled in with a favorite book. It was comfort, and it was home.

For a moment, he wanted nothing more than to remain here. Always.

Marisol's eyes wandered the cavern, searching the curve of the walls and the lip of every pool. The multi-colored liquid in each strange basin gently kissed the edge of its container, sometimes threatening to break free of its assigned perimeter, but never fully cresting that border. As they stepped forward, her gaze was drawn to one specific pool. She thought only to glance for a moment, but found herself unable to pull away from the hypnotic visions within.

Lives played out before her within the confines of the pool's assigned surface. They flashed before her in rapid succession. Hundreds upon hundreds of lived experiences played out within moments. Young, old, rich, poor, from the greatest statesman to the vilest villain, each was a glimpse of their last moments. With each blink, more lives passed before her. They were endless and unknowable. Yet some part of her recognized these were stories of lives past and wondered where she might find her own.

"Draw your eyes away child," a soothing voice broke her trance, "Those visions are not meant for the eyes of others, much less the eyes of the dead." said the voice. Suddenly, she felt very cold. As if the words bored into the core of her being with the chill of winter itself.

The voice echoed all around her, but she knew at once its source.

The figure that had been tending the pools.

They had both assumed the figure to be larger than it was. A trick of the light, or a change in reflection from the myriad of liquids around them, perhaps? Had it been standing? Or seated? It moved slowly now, toward an elevated cap of stone between several pools. It slowly clambered to the top and sat down, the pole resting across its lap as it watched them both. It made no other sound.

The eyes of the entity watched them both as they continued their methodical approach. They seemed at once the eyes of a child, but the weight of knowledge hidden behind them was too heavy for the slender limbs of youth to carry. These were the eyes of youth long forgotten, who had witnessed joy burn and fade. They were the eyes of wisdom coming to the acceptance that they truly knew nothing. They were eyes of pain and joy, of levity and horror. They were the eyes that welcomed the face of a newborn, and the red-rimmed eyes of the grief-stricken widow.

It was both ageless and without gender, this strange entity in the hallowed hall of the dead. Perhaps it was an illusion, crafted by the magicks of others. Or perhaps it was crafted by The Barrows itself. Whatever its origins, it was certainly not human. And it was certainly not mortal.

The entity shifted slightly on its rock-hewn perch and looked up at Emilio. Behind the entity stood a large oval, carved into the rough facade of the cavern wall. Its surface was slick and black, like wet onyx. Light cast shadows around them, strange whispers of dancing darkness. They could make out their own reflections in the slick stone, but the entity bore no such reflection in the shiny surface, and no shadow danced on the surrounding ground.

Emilio considered the small entity for a moment. Even with the altered sight he currently possessed, he could not discern the truth of the creature. It was an illusion, or it was of this place entirely, something as fundamental as the stone beneath his feet or the air in his lungs.

He had felt the entity's words as it spoke to Marisol. They had echoed in his bones. Whatever this creature was, it was more than anything Emilio had ever encountered in the past. It was fascinating, and terrifying.

The pair stood before the seated child thing and waited.

The child-like entity considered them both and then spoke. Its words felt heavy with age and power.

"Life begets Death and Death begets Life," its voice sounded across the cavern and sang in their veins. "A sacred river of molten stone, birthed from the heart of the world, seeped from these caverns in ages past. I was here to witness its birth." The entity turned its ancient gaze to Marisol. "When the pressures of time brought forth the need of this space to labor and in its labor bring forth both destruction and new life, I was the author of its pain."

Marisol swallowed hard and grasped Emilio's hand tightly.

The figure's eyes slid to Emilio.

"Long before mankind walked the broken and brittle rocks along these shores, have I guarded The Barrows Way. When the earth cooled, and your people sought places of power hoping to become more than what the Gods made them to be, I was here."

The figure lifted the pole from its lap and gestured to the tunnel behind them.

"When mankind came, crawling from the darkness, seeking control over concepts they could never understand, they found me. Discontent with what they had leeched from the veins of the earth, they, who thought they had mastered Death itself, came here, seeking yet more."

Shadows danced around them and the air felt chill. The entity stood slowly. Effortlessly. Was it taller now?

"Driven by hubris, they tapped the very veins of Death itself and drew that power into themselves. They sought to rule the fleeting world of flesh by living without the glorious burden of Time. They would mold Death to their desires and become immortal while wearing mortal form."

The entity chuckled darkly.

"I allowed them their delusions, for I knew that greed would be their undoing."

The entity locked eyes with Emilio. He was fixed in place as the thing stared into the depths of his very being. His chest constricted as if compressed by the pressure of a hundred icy hands. The air was forced from his lungs.

"And it was."

It blinked, and Emilio was released. He fell to his knees on the cavern floor, Marisol kneeling at his side.

"There is one thing that overcomes the greed of a human soul," it said.

"Fear." it looked down at Emilio and Marisol. "I needed to do nothing but wait, and they would turn upon themselves. Greed begetting fear, begetting greed."

It bowed its head a moment, and the shadows danced higher. Emilio blinked, and it was no longer standing atop its stone seat. Instead, it stood at the foot of the onyx oval, fingers gently caressing its edge. In the fading light, it looked like a frozen onyx pool, laying upright on the cavern wall.

"They eventually fell to others of humankind...misguided and greedy... each of them, seeking the same grandeur... and lies... of the Necromancers of the past. If you knock, you can still hear their pleas," the figure paused and rapped lightly on its surface with a bare-knuckle.

The still air was suddenly filled with cries of terror and sorrow. Each asking for their forgiveness, longing to be free. Emilio felt his blood run cold, and Marisol's hands covered her mouth in horror.

"Shhhh," the figure whispered to the voices softly, and then gently caressed the pool's onyx surface. A deafening silence filled the empty void. The creature bowed its head a moment and then slowly turned back to Emilio.

"I bear no name other than this place I guard. So tell me, young Necromancer ... what power do you seek from Barrows Way? Speak!" the entity commanded.

"We seek an audience with a Barrows Scholar," Emilio blurted in response, overcome with urgency. His hands leapt to cover his lips, but the words were pulled from him by forces beyond his control.

The entity pursed its lips and considered a moment before it spoke.

"Those that you seek are no more young Necromancer. They were slain in these hallowed halls. Their only sin was gullibility," the figure's shoulders rose and fell in a noncommittal shrug. "They believed the twisted truth of those that do not understand the beauty of their god's light. That was their folly."

The figure of Styx-made-flesh walked away from the onyx portal and toward the edge of a nearby pool. Reaching out, they held their hand out over its multicolored surface. Pictures and memories played out in the liquid surface.

"Their spirits lingered here and, as all things are, were eventually drawn to me. I offered them an answer to any question that they wished," the pictures in the pool settled on images of several sets of eyes, each looking out of the water, searching for answers. The figure waved its fingers, and the images vanished.

"They could have asked for anything, instead they all asked the same question ...each one and all." The avatar of Death turned back to the pair once more, "I answered truthfully and in doing so freed them from the bonds of magic their murderers held upon their souls. They were allowed to leave this place for the next."

"You have come to speak with scholars who no longer have voices in this realm." the entity said plainly.

It was as if the very breath was kicked out of him. The strength in his legs failed and Emilio slumped to the ground. Surrounded by the riches of eternal knowledge, the power of the realm of Entropy at his fingertips, but it was all pointless. An avatar of Styx stood before him, in one of the most sacred of spaces, but it was without meaning now. He felt empty.

He had failed.

With sorrowful eyes, he looked up at his Queen, "I'm ... I'm sorry. I promised, and I failed... I failed you, Marisol... forgive me," he pleaded as the weight of defeat crashed over him.

Marisol knelt by Emilio and took his face into her hands. "No. Never." she whispered and gently wiped away his tears with her thumbs. "You did not fail me Emilio. Never, never believe that. You did not fail me."

"Why?" the avatar asked. It was a simple question, without an immediate answer.

The power of its tone commanded Emilio's attention. He lifted his chin and looked up at the entity.

"What knowledge does a Scholar of the Barrow's hold that drives you so? What power over death have you come to find from the ghosts of the departed?"

Slowly Emilio rose back to his feet, "I do not come here seeking power. I do not come asking for myself." he swallowed hard and met the shadowy eyes of the entity before him. "I would be a liar to say that I don't have questions. I have many, many questions - but I came here seeking the wisdom and knowledge to save this woman. To reunite her body with her spirit. She has been robbed of her life."

The entity stared at him, and Emilio could feel his mind open. Unasked questions upon his soul being reviewed by the eyes of eternity.

"As have thousands of others." the entity responded.

"I do not ask for thousands of others. I ask for this... single... soul."

The Guardian grew silent as ancient eyes regarded them. Ancient eyes turned to Marisol. Eyes that invoked terror on the living brought only awe and elation, comfort and consolation.

I can release you now if you wish. The Guardian's voice sounded soft in her mind. *This world is no longer your concern.*

I am not ready yet; she answered honestly.

There was silence for a heartbeat, and then it replied, *No, you are not.*

"There is a cost." it spoke to them both.

"I will pay it." Marisol offered.

The Guardian held up a warning finger. "It is not a cost the dead may pay." They looked at Emilio once more. "You have paid dearly twice already, young necromancer. I can see it on your soul. Will you pay a third time?"

Emilio straightened his shoulders and met the creature's gaze.

"Emilio, no..." Marisol cautioned.

"So much bravery in the face of the unknown..." the Guardian mused. In a single fluid motion, it gestured toward the contents of the nearby pool. Mirror-like fluid floated from its surface into the hands of the Guardian. It leaned forward then, and whispered words of ancient power into the fluid. Words that burned the air and chilled the heart. When shape finally came to the fluid's form, what was left behind was a small round disc the size of a human palm. The edges of the disc were decorated with the same designs seen in the entryway hall.

He held the disc out to Emilio.

"What is this?" he asked as he carefully accepted the offered token.

"What you seek." the Guardian replied. It released the token and looked at the pair. Power washed over them both with its words.

"Life begets Death and Death begets Life. Between Hil, Geekind and Styx, the balance must be maintained in all things. This is the agreement. The cycle of the world. Marisol Ambrosia Failla has been removed from this world. With that clay token, her soul may be restored to its mortal form, with love and sacrifice. Snap the token in twain and she will return to the world above."

Emilio stared at the token in his hands. It was everything they had come for.

"What is the sacrifice?" Marisol interrupted. "What is the cost?"

The Guardian smiled at her words. "The balance must be paid. A life for a life. A soul for a soul. She may return to the world, but someone must take her place."

"No." Marisol gasped.

Emilio nodded and stared at the token in his hands. "I understand."

The Guardian chuckled darkly. It sounded like stone grating on stone. "It is not that easy, young necromancer. It will not be you who takes her place. Someone somewhere will die. It may be someone known to the token holder, or it may be a complete stranger. However, the stain of that murder will be marked on their soul."

The shock of the declaration rocked both Emilio and Marisol. Just as both were about to protest, the Guardian continued, "The soul in question cannot and will not influence the decision of the token breaker. The Dead cannot influence the Living in this. It is their choice and their choice alone. The dead do not carry the weight of the living."

The finality of the Guardian's words felt like a chain being locked in place on Marisol's soul.

The pair looked at one another and knew at that moment, this was the only way. It would have to be a life for a life.

RETRIBUTION

The travelers made their way across the great columned chamber in silence. While they were observed by dozens of eyes, none made any motions towards them outside of a bow of deference. At the entrance, one creature cloaked in shadow sat. Emilio stared at the creature for a few moments, and then it bowed in kind before making its way back into the shadows beyond.

Crossing over the threshold once again, Marisol slowly rubbed her hands together. The sensation of feeling cold was gone. She looked at the entrance again and sighed.

Emilio stopped a few feet from her when he realized she was no longer at his side. Watching her, he understood and gave a saddened smile. Whispering a few words, he held out his hand to her. A familiar blue glow surrounded him once more.

She turned and grasped his hand. It differed from before.

Emilio nodded, and he turned to make his way toward the far pinpoint of light. The revelation of the Guardian still weighed heavily on their souls. A life for a life, whether it was known or unknown, felt heavy, and a burden that neither wished upon anyone.

The journey seemed shorter than their initial trek, but it was made in silence. He wanted to say something to her as they walked, but he could not find the words. To bring her back, someone had to die. He wanted to shout how awful and terrible it was, but there was no one to argue with. One does not argue or bargain with Death. Death was the end of all things, even in its kindest moments.

The avatar of Styx, a facet of Death itself, had given them kindness, an opportunity to right a wrong ... with another wrong. His thoughts were full of argument and conflict, but he kept it all bottled away as he held her hand. Eventually, he would need to let her go, but at this moment, her touch was the only thing keeping him focused.

From out of the foul miasma-filled labyrinth, Emilio trudged his way up the hill with Marisol in hand. The horse they had left behind was still tied to its post. They crested the top of the hill, and were met by half a dozen riders and too many muzzles pointed at him from the walls beyond. That realization was followed by more than a dozen rifles slotting their bolts in response.

Their bluff had been called.

A shot rang out, and Emilio was slammed backward. The spooked horses pulled at their reigns as a single voice shouted, "HOLD YOUR FIRE! I DID NOT GIVE THE COMMAND TO FIRE!"

Wide-eyed, Marisol fell to her knees at Emilio's side. "Emilio!"

The slug had gone through his armor like butter. He let out a deep, but pained breath and placed his hand on his chest. But there was no blood. A flash of green light caught his eye. The ground beneath him bore a faint and familiar greenish glow.

Was the land protecting them?

He moved to stand.

"DOCTOR EMILIO KANE - RAISE YOUR HANDS IN THE AIR!" shouted a voice in the distance.

"Oh, my gods Lykos! What are you doing?!" Marisol shouted. Only Emilio could hear her.

Emilio surveyed the surrounding scene. Mounted riders and footmen. Too many to avoid, too many to fight. King Lykos Eskill, "Queen" Marisol, three of the Gran Salón's Guard, and Kalidah - stripped of her armor with head cast down, were all mounted. One rider had a pistol trained on her while the other two stared at him with hatred. Along the wall, some soldiers had their rifles partly trained on him - the others had their sights aimed behind him.

They were expecting a horde to come over the hill.

The Queen's doppelgänger had made its play.

"Your Majesty, if I may ..." Emilio started.

"You may NOT," shouted Lykos. " Doctor Kane, we have never met, though I have been aware of your presence within The Reach. My father knew of you, and he choose to tolerate your presence, because he found you useful. When I assumed my position and you were made known to me, I too did nothing because I was assured you were not a threat, and your presence was a boon for my kingdom.

"Your presence was even endorsed by Captain Chandra. It was because of her we referred several troubled families to your care. All of this seemed an amicable and quiet relationship. One that I was willing to tolerate. But apparently, your kind and beneficent demeanor was all a lie! All of this was simply a means for you to beguile the Captain of the Gran Salón, and have her BETRAY HER HONOR so you could gain access to this unholy place!"

Lykos stared past the Necromist to the land beyond him. His face was full of disgust.

"I have no words for what you have done, Doctor Kane, nor do I trust you with anything that could come out of your mouth. Look at yourself! Even your very appearance betrays the unholy work you have engaged in! Whatever godless power you gained from this place may have saved your life from an overexcited marksman, but I would wager that power will not last long. You are an unnatural thing, Doctor Kane, and your time here is finished." He sat up straighter in his saddle and stared down at Emilio. "Maybe Hil's Inquisition can burn the lies out of your tongue. The Reach no longer wishes to hear your lies." He gestured to the footmen. "Guards! Bind and gag him. If he says another word or makes any untoward motion, shoot him."

Emilio hung his head. There was nothing he could do. If he moved, the sharpshooters would make short work of him. If it was just his life at stake, he would not have cared. He and those of his kind had been hated by the world at large. It was a hatred he was used to bearing. But he was not alone in this. Kalidah had been disgraced for her part in this. If he died, Marisol would lose any chance of returning to her life. All he could do was stand with his hands in the air and hope that Styx or any of the other Gods of this world were watching and took pity on his plight.

Forcing him to his knee with a hard swat from a rifle butt, Emilio gave no resistance to the two guards. Around his head came a strap that held a foul metal gag. They could have easily broken his teeth by forcing it in, but he gave them no opportunity for cruelty as held his mouth open wide. The metal plug tasted foul, and he wanted to gag, but forced himself to breathe deeply through his nose. He felt his arms forced back as his arms and hands were bound. While he couldn't see it, he knew what they were using. A pair of metal rods that ended in a metal glove on each. His hands were slid in, giving them no room for motion. Someone with smaller hands might have some wiggle room, but for him, the gloves pinched tight. These restraints were made to subdue those who could wield magic, courtesy of the Inquisitors of Hil.

Marisol was not deterred by the detachment in front of her. She was shocked at the response, and horrified at Emilio's treatment. She had seen Lykos angry in the past, and she could tell he was absolutely furious. Her eyes fell on the creature wearing her likeness. It sat tall and smug next to the King. A look of gloating satisfaction painted on its well mimicked features. No doubt Lykos' fury was stoked by her actions. The presence of the creature fueled Marisol's resolve. She knew what she had to do.

Emilio had risked his life to save her, so she could do no less to save him.

Undeterred by the soldiers, Marisol made her way to Kalidah. She floated up to her friend, "Kalidah - can you hear me?"

There was no response.

She took a breath and thought of Emilio's words - *a Spirit - with basic focus could manifest just their voice, or enough force to move an object...*

Focus. She needed to focus on what she wanted to do.

The hot pool of red energy within her came ready to the surface. She wanted to use her rage against the target of her vengeance. She swallowed it down. She could not tap that strength. Emilio had cautioned her against its use. No. She had to focus on herself.

"... Kalidah ..."

Kalidah opened her eyes. The tears on her face were not tears of anguish or sorrow. They were tears of anger. She was furious. When confronted with her actions, she had no proof. No evidence upon which to justify her claims. She had stolen from her king and aided in the impersonation of an Inquisitor. All to aid a pariah she had called a friend. A person of dangerous background, seeking access to one of the most heavily guarded areas of the Kingdom. All of this on little more than his word. Her actions were suspect. She was suspect.

They had stripped her of armor, weapons, and title. Like Emilio Kane, she was now an outcast.

"Kalidah! Can you hear me?"

The ointment Emilio had given her had already dried away, but Kalidah knew her Queen's voice. Without a word, she gave a slight nod.

"I will grab your guard's pistol, but you need to grab their sword. Once that is done, you need to let me in ... I will do the rest."

Instinct told her to say no, but the command of her sovereign and friend overrode that. She glanced to her right, noting the position of the guard, and again to the left, marking his partner. One had their pistol trained on her, the other was ready with a blade. She would need to make this count. Relaxing her shoulders, Kalidah took a deep breath and closed her eyes.

"Let come what may."

Reaching out with willed force, Marisol slapped the pistol out of the guard's hand. The pistol flew out of the shocked guard's grasp and went flying overhead. Shouts of concern followed at the sight of the flying firearm. At the distraction, Marisol gripped the guard's sword and pulled it out of its sheath just as Lykos' words condemned Emilio to the Inquisitors.

Kalidah swiftly dismounted to face her shocked guard. Extending her arm, she grabbed the sword from the air.

Marisol floated forward, chanting the words she heard the Necromist speak before. A familiar sensation filled her body as she became one with Kalidah. Opening her eyes, she fixed her gaze on the creature that wore her likeness. Her fingers wrapped around the grip of the saber.

With reckless abandon, Kalidah/Marisol looked over to the Queen and attacked her.

The Queen dodged the hasty blow, narrowly avoiding the sharpened blade of the former captain.

"Are you insane woman?!" The Queen called.

Kalidah/Marisol swung again, this time striking the flat of the blade against the Queen's horse. It reared in complaint. She fumbled with the reins and fell, tumbling to the ground.

Soldiers and guardsmen quickly attempted to retrain their firearms on new targets. Two guards attempting to target Emilio fired wide, missing the necromist entirely. Too much unexpected activity and the need to avoid hitting the Queen impacting their aim.

The Queen's horse galloped away, and she backed up closer to the King. She quickly drew the King's blade from his saddlebag.

"Treason AND attempted Murder Chandra?" the Queen declared.

Lykos' guards formed up around him as best as they could.

Emilio remained unmoved, eyes wide as the spectacle unfolded.

"Her name is Kalidah Chandra," said Kalidah/Marisol. Their overlapped voices sounded out. The Queen's eyes widened in panic.

Lykos frowned suddenly in confusion.

Using Kalidah's frame, Marisol made several powerful slashes at the Queen, forcing her on the defensive. The Queen brought her blade up to block the blows. Marisol advanced.

"Lykos - my love! That is not your Queen. This monstrosity is a mimic who murdered me and is planning the ruin of The Reach!" Kalidah's voice overlapped with Marisol's as they kept swinging the blade downward.

"Lykos! Don't just sit there like an idiot, order your men to shoot this traitor!" the Queen said as she continued to block each strike.

The look of confusion was clear on Lykos' face.

Marisol refused to be deterred, "You are disgusted with lizards losing their tails because of an incident you had when you were nine. The bastard thing left its tail in your hand, still wiggling, and it gave your nightmares for weeks!" Kalidah/Marisol said.

Lykos' eyes went wide at the declaration. He pointed at the former captain as she brought her blade down once more on the figure of the Queen.

"PROTEC ... Kalidah ... Marisol!" he commanded.

"YES, MY LOVE!" Kalidah/Marisol said but soon found themselves reeling back. With the King's sword, the Queen began a series of rapid slashes that made Kalidah/Marisol shift into a defensive stance. "That is NOT your Queen! It is a mimic with ambitions of disaster!"

"I am NO MIMIC!" the Queen shouted as she continued her onslaught.

Emilio watched as everything transpired before him. Any attempt at protest from him would lead to a volley of gunfire. If anyone could save Marisol, it would be herself.

Continuing to use Kalidah's raw strength, Marisol switched her stance to purely offensive. With several heavy and quick blows, she wore down the Queen's defensive pose enough to get one strike in. The blow was quick enough to bypass the Queen's defense and allowed Marisol to score a hit across the Queen's right cheek. The blade slashed across the Queen's face, sending hot BLUE fluid in the air that slapped into Lyko's face.

Reaching up to touch his face, Lykos looked at his palm and saw brackish blue blood on his hand. He wiped the unnatural-looking fluid from his face in disgust. Realizing the horror of what had transpired, he took out his pistol and tried to aim at the Queen.

The fighting between the Captain of the Guard and the imposter rose to a heated fury as both individuals continued to exchange deadly blows. Marisol felt her time running out as her control over Kalidah's body became more and more sluggish. She needed to end it now. Allowing her own lessons to take hold, she slid forward on her knee, using Kalidah's frame and bulk to propel her forward. Dropping her foot, she forced a pivot as she brought up her sword to deflect the Queen's downward strike. The weight of her momentum kept her going forward, and around the Queen. With one strike, she slashed the Queen's calves to bring her down. Unnaturally, the Queen's torso twisted to face her with a face full of rage. Springing up, Kalidah/Marisol swung and slashed the Queen's sword-bearing arm. Then raised her fist and slammed her left hand into the face of the Queen. Kalidah Chandra was a powerful woman, and her body packed a powerful punch. Any man or woman would have found themselves floored by the blow, but the Queen only reeled back slightly with a hiss. The impression of Kalidah's fist was stamped into the Queen's face.

Kalidah/Marisol rushed forward then, bringing their shoulder into the Queen's chest and knocking her back to the ground. She followed her body's momentum and leaped forward, planting her knees into her stomach.

Faster than expected, the Queen pulled out a hidden blade from her sleeve and stabbed Kalidah/Marisol in the ribs repeatedly. Enraged, Kalidah/Marisol grabbed the Queen's hand, the offending weapon still lodged in her side. With her free hand, she pulled back and struck the Queen in the face.

Again and again.

Lykos and the guards stared in horror.

The creature that was not the Queen howled in pain and anger, unable to free itself, but desperate to hold its form despite the oncoming violence. Kalidah/Marisol beat the creature, yelling about the horrors of being smothered alive and having to experience dying. Each time she struck, more brackish blue blood spread and sprayed all over.

Strength soon left the creature as Kalidah/Marisol's onslaught seemed never-ending. With its exhausted final breath, the creature spoke in an unnatural voice, "HE will come for you all - whether to the East or the North. He will seek to claim all of this ... even the dead...".

And then it was no more.

When it ceased moving, Kalidah/Marisol slumped forward and fell to the side.

An unseen observer in the mountain range watched as it all unfolded. They leaned on their long pole and turned ageless eyes from the spectacle and wandered back into the shadows.

THE CHOICE

Everything happened at once.

Emilio struggled against the gag and against the bindings. The guards focused their attention on the combatants and were no longer on him. He watched as Kalidah/Marisol eventually stood up from the mess of blood and held her own gut. They staggered.

Turning towards the King, they spoke "Lykos, get this woman..." and Marisol fell backward out of her friend. Kalidah fell to her knees, trying to catch her breath. "Release that man, Your Majesty. We're running out of time," she said.

Lykos felt the eyes on him, and quickly dismounted. "You heard your captain, free him now!" he commanded and turned to the wall, "DO NOT EVEN THINK OF FIRING!" he shouted, "SEND OUT A HEALER NOW!"

Lykos knelt by Kalidah. "I am so sorry, I..."

Kalidah shook her head and held up her hand to show that Lykos should pause. She ran her tongue across her teeth and then turned her head to spit blood. "Forgive me when I say this ...but... save It, your Majesty." she said in pained words. She nodded in Emilio's direction. "I am not dying today. Talk to Kane."

Emilio felt the binds loosen, and his hands were freed. The metal gag was pulled from his mouth. His mouth and nose filled with the smell of combat mixed with murder. He wretched. Spitting the taste out of his mouth, he pushed himself up from his hands and knees and stood.

A long shadow passed over him. He looked up and into the eyes of the King.

"Explain quickly Kane."

Emilio nodded and wiped his hands on his leather pants. " Of course, Sire. Your wife was murdered by a doppelgänger," he gestured to the malformed pile of blue flesh that used to be the Queen, "Her Spirit found me. I realized the creature had to be keeping your wife in some form of magical preservation. I believed there may be a way to reunite her soul with her body. We came here," Emilio said with conviction. It was brief, but true.

"Did you find it?" Lykos asked.

"We did," Emilio said and then looked around. He saw Marisol's form on the ground. A thin green tendril streaked along the ground from her to him.

"Shit!" he exclaimed and then apologized. "I'm sorry, your Majesty, please excuse me." and stepped around the King. Rushing to the Spirit of the Queen, he knelt and his arms beneath her small form. She was unconscious, but did not appear as drained as she had been previously. Emilio felt hopeful at that observation. He rose, taking her into his arms, her head resting on his shoulder. Turning around, he looked at Lykos. "We need to get back to Gran Salón before sunset. If this creature was preserving her body, that magic may not hold now that it is dead. I don't know how much longer we have, sir."

Lykos watched the Necromist holding the air that was his wife's soul. If it were not for where they currently stood, he would have believed none of it. He raised his hand and flagged down a guard.

"You! Yes, you. I need transport for Doctor Kane immediately!" he paused and looked at Kane. "Can you ride like that?"

"No Majesty."

Lykos turned back to the guard. " Don't just stand there, man, see if this damn place has what he needs." He glowered at the wall. "OPEN THOSE GATES AND WHERE IS THAT DAMN HEALER!!"

The gates opened, and a pair dressed in medical uniform ran out and tended to Kalidah's injuries. Looking up at him, she said nothing, but gave him a nod. They would see each other again, but for now, he had to say goodbye.

He looked down at Marisol as he cradled her in his arms. "Hang in there, please."

Things soon after became a blur of motion as Emilio was helped into a small wagon. Normally used for foodstuff, today it sped along bearing him and the unseen spirit of Marisol. The gates opened, and the royal entourage, along with Emilio, raced their way back to the Gran Salón at top speed. As the countryside flew by, none of it registered to Emilio. His world in this moment was one Spirit, laying on the flat of a wagon. His hand in hers, he held onto her for fear of her drifting away.

Chaos erupted at their arrival at just before two in the afternoon. Striding into the Salón, Lykos ordered the staff and guard to search the place from top to bottom. All of it was done with a single grim order ... if it was big enough to hold the body of a woman, open it up.

Just after four, Marisol awoke. Spirits did not need to sleep as mortals did, but the actions she had taken drained her. She sat up in the wagon and listened as Emilio caught her up about what had transpired since the events of the outpost.

Looking about, she noted the shades of the guards had taken position around the wagon.

"When they saw you, they took up their posts to ensure you would be okay," Emilio said.

Marisol nodded to each of them. "Thank you."

"It is our honor, your Majesty."

A blood-curdling scream emerged from inside the Salón. The shades drew sword and shield, and stood at the ready.

Emilio looked at Marisol, "I think they found your body, your Majesty."

They were led into a private courtyard far from the front walls. Lykos, the guards, and a few of the house staff surrounded a figure wrapped in a sheet, laying on a stone bench. Fascination and nervousness filled the eyes of both staff and guards at Emilio's approach. They glanced up at him and then looked away.

Am I really that disturbing to look at? Sighing, he made his way to the bench.

The figure lay there with the sheet pulled over it. He had seen this display many times in many morgues during his studies. It was a symbol of respect for the dead.

"They found her body inside the bed in the Queen's private chambers. The creature had removed the mattress and broken the supporting frame enough to place the body in the center. It has been sleeping on top of her all this time," Lykos said. The shock and turmoil of the entire experience was evident upon his face. The accusations of a few hours prior were more real. He turned his pained gaze to Emilio, "It is your turn Doctor, what can we do?"

Emilio nodded and gestured to the figure. "May I?" he asked.

Lykos agreed.

"Thank you." Emilio stepped over to the side of the figure and pulled the sheet back to reveal Queen Marisol's mortal form. She was still in her bedclothes. Looking down at her face, Emilio could see faint red impressions over her nose and mouth. He leaned in to examine them for a moment and then stood back up. It looked as if it only just happened. There was no bruising or discoloration. She had been preserved within moments of her death. The question was how.

"Your Majesty, I need to employ a rite to see what is keeping her body in this state. Will you allow me to do so?"

"Proceed, Doctor," was all Lykos said.

"Hil's Light, grant me sight!" Emilio spoke softly. Invoking the Vista once again. He opened his eyes and saw the body of the Queen glow with a greenish-silvery light. The power was a sleeve over her form, but the source seem to originate from her right hand.

"That isn't mine," Marisol said. She could see the power coming off of the ring, but she could not understand it. "Is that keeping me ... like that?"

Pulling the sheet aside, Emilio lifted her right hand to examine it. A strange power emanated from the ring on her hand. The ring appeared to be gold with a whitish inlay. Glyphs were inscribed along the inlay, as well as etched into the rest of the ring. Staring deeper into the flow of the power, Emilio saw glyphs wrapping around her body. He placed her hand back beside her prone figure.

He understood it all now.

Nodding his head, he turned back to the King. The sun had disappeared behind some dark clouds on the horizon. Rain was coming once again. He looked around the courtyard. There were too many people here. Too many stories to be told, and too much judgment from those that do not understand.

"Your Majesty, what I tell you is for your ears only."

Looking around, Lykos understood. "Everyone, back to places. Liam, see that everything is in order."

The Head of Staff gave a quick bow and clapped his hands. "You heard his Majesty, put this house back into order. If I catch anyone eavesdropping or speaking of this, there will be Hell to pay."

The guards made their way inside, except for one who stood by the archway and was out of earshot. Turning back to the Necromist, Lykos said, "You have the floor, Doctor Kane."

He did not want to do this. Despite the incident and words earlier, Lykos Eskill was a good man. He did not deserve this, nor did he deserve this kind of choice.

"The ring is preserving the Queen's body. The enchantment was not tied to the life of the doppelgänger, so its death does not threaten the enchantment. We have time, if we want it," he looked to Lykos and delivered the information as he might any other medical prognosis. It was careful and measured and designed to not invoke emotion from the family. It was also very difficult.

"Should the ring be removed, the natural processes that are currently held in stasis will begin. The magics that are halting those processes are based in this ring. Once it is removed, it cannot be undone. Placing it back upon her once removed will not restart the process." he paused a moment and continued.

"You may choose this option, sire, and let your wife go. She avenged her death with the help of Captain Chandra. When she is laid to rest, her Spirit will move on from this world to the next. I could not tell you where that is, only that she will now be able to do so. She cannot, however, move on unless that ring is removed." Emilio said.

"Wait, I thought you said there was a way to save her? I don't understand," Lykos asked.

Emilio considered the man standing before him. He could simply choose to not tell him. The ring would keep her body in stasis for as long as needed. He could go back to the Academy. The Lecturer and the Scribe might know something. There might be another way. He wanted there to be another way. Despite all his desires, he knew there wasn't. Barrows Hall would have told him if there had been. This was all there was.

He could not omit the truth. A lie of omission was still a lie. The dead had no reason to lie, and neither could he.

Looking toward Marisol, he saw she stood on the other side of the bench. He watched her look at Lykos, her own body, and then back to Emilio. She nodded her head. "In The Barrows, I discovered a way to save her, yes." Emilio began.

"Well, out with it then! Tell me what needs to be done!"

Emilio held his hand up, asking for the King's patience. "It is a difficult thing to say, and I have to be honest with you, sir. You will not like it." Closing his eyes, Emilio took a deep breath and then pulled out a small velvet pouch. Opening the pouch, he withdrew the small clay disc. In the light outside The Barrows, it looked like a coin.

He offered it to Lykos.

"A sacrifice must be paid. By snapping this disc in two, her soul will instantly be restored to her body. However, where there is life, there is death, and a balance must be made. Someone somewhere will die. It may be someone known to you or a complete stranger. However, the stain of that murder will be marked on your soul."

The lingering shock had faded, and realization hit him across the face. "Wait what?" Lykos said. A myriad of emotions passed behind the King's eyes: horror, disbelief, suffering, grief.

Emilio explained the cost of the token once more. As he did, the darkened sky above let loose a light drizzle. Emilio held out the disc to the King once more and Lykos cautiously took it from his hand and studied it.

Looking back, he stared at the face of his Queen. "She looks like she is asleep. Like she could wake up any moment," he said as he wiped the moisture from her face and cupped her cheek.

Across from him, Marisol wept without tears. She was without voice or action in this. In the disc's presence, she was rooted to the ground and unable to speak. The rules of the Guardian were clear, the dead could not influence the decision of the living. She could only watch as this played out.

With his free hand, Lykos brushed away the raindrops from her eyes. His attention was hers and he did not look at Emilio when he spoke.

"I am a peace-time king, Kane. I'm not my father. King Raphael charged into battle with his men to secure the borders of The Reach from raiders. I am not a soldier. I have never taken a life. I am a diplomat. My wars have always been fought with words I've never... I've never taken a life."

He looked back at Emilio, and demanded, "Who told you all this? Who gave you this accursed thing?"

The words sounded angry, but Emilio knew what spoken pain sounded like. He knew those in pain, in grief. All they needed was an opportunity for release. Anger was part of the process. Both emotions were fighting for control. Emilio had dealt with this conflict too many times to count when he counseled those that sought his help. Lykos deserved that same sympathy.

"An avatar of the god Styx," Emilio said.

"Oh," was the only reply. It was the only reply there could be. Lykos paused and looked at the disc in his hand, then up to the sky above and to the ground below. "What does she want me to do?" he asked, looking at the Queen's body.

"Her Majesty may not express an opinion. The Dead cannot influence the Will of the Living. That was the binding rule of the token."

"Is she here now?" he asked.

"She is your Majesty. She cannot speak, but she is here," Emilio said. His eyes went to where Marisol stood, weeping and watching as her husband wrestled with the weight of the choice before him.

Lykos Eskill was not a war hawk. He was a diplomat and mediator. He was everything a king should be without bloodshed. He was being asked to take a life to save hers. She was forbidden words at this moment, but Emilio knew all she wanted to do was hold him, and tell him it would be okay. That it was okay. He did not have to do this.

Lykos cleared his throat and stared at the clay coin in his hand. The price of Marisol's soul.

"This person could be someone who was already dying, or a criminal, even someone who deserved to die," Lykos said as he held the disc.

"They could, your Majesty." Emilio replied. "Or It could also be a newborn, a child, a mother, an innocent."

"Someone who doesn't deserve this." Lykos whispered. He paused and looked over at Emilio then, "She ... she loved ... loves The Reach. She loves the people, and their willingness to cultivate the land, not just for the sake of food, but because it ensured that the land thrived. She always thought that the land here was lucky to have the people appreciate it. I think the people and the land were lucky enough to have her. I was lucky that she said yes."

Whether it was the drizzle or tears, Lykos wiped his face with his sleeve. He turned back to the body of the Queen and knelt by her side, then placed the disc on her chest above her heart. Then he took her hand in his and held it.

Lykos held his wife's hand. "I love you, Marisol. I cannot imagine what you have gone through to get here; to get to this moment. In all the time we have been together, I know you would not have wanted this. You would not want someone to die for you. I don't think you would forgive yourself or me if I brought you back this way."

Marisol felt the binds on her soul loosen. He had made his choice. Even without tears, she sobbed.

Gripping the strange ring, Lykos slid it off her finger and placed it on the disc. "Forgive me for not saving you."

Marisol slumped forward, holding herself against the bench. On the other side, Lykos leaned over her body and allowed himself to grieve.

Quietly, Emilio reached over and took both items off of the Queen's body and placed them back in his pouch. Looking over at Lykos, he placed a hand on the King's shoulder, "I'm sorry for your loss. She will be forever remembered."

Lykos did not look up, but reached over and gripped Emilio's hand. "Thank you for trying," he whispered. Squeezing it once, he let go, and the Necromist stood back. Turning out of the courtyard, he walked back inside to give the King and Queen their time to grieve.

THE JOURNEY HOME

Emilio was alone in a small waiting room that normally housed various visitors and dignitaries. There were a few small tables, a few comfortable chairs, and a couch that he almost fell asleep on. For the first hour, he sat alone with his thoughts. Liam Stack, the Head of Staff checked on him periodically and ensured that he had something to eat and drink while he waited. Unsure of what to do, he took the time to write a letter to Kalidah. It rambled on for several pages, with him apologizing for everything and thanking her for what she had done. The letter ultimately ended with an offer of a visit on her terms. Liam entered the room once more as Emilio finished the letter. He was carrying several odd boxes.

"His Majesty has requested a Guild coach to return you to Knot's End. It should be here relatively soon. Given the state of your person, sir, I would recommend this," Liam said. He opened up one box. Inside was a flat, long-brimmed hat he handed to Emilio.

"Is it that bad?" Emilio asked, regarding his new hair color.

"It is a very fashion-forward statement, sir, but one I am uncertain The Reach is ready to embrace."

"Hrmm. Well spoken." Emilio nodded. A lock of stone white hair on one side of his head was exceedingly strange, but half his head? He settled the hat atop his crown.

"Very fetching, sir." Liam noted, "Certifiably Spooky."

Emilio smiled, "Well, I did graduate with top marks from Fugue."

Liam continued. "Second, sir, His Majesty understands that your services usually bear a fee of some sort. As you were technically under the employ of the late Queen, it is only right that you be paid for services rendered to the Crown."

Emilio opened his mouth to protest, but was stopped with a single glance from Liam.

"I have been ordered to instruct you that if you do not accept this, you may find it shackled to you all the way back home," Liam said with a semi-serious but caring smile as he handed over a small iron box.

Emilio opened it up and felt a twinge of guilt. The amount within was several times more than made in a single year. He looked up to protest.

Liam waved his hand away. "Believe me, son, just take it."

Emilio sighed and simply nodded his head as he shut the box. "Mr. Stack, can you do me a small favor? I know she is recovering from her injuries, but when she returns, can you give this to Captain Chandra? You probably want to wait until she is in a good enough mood to appreciate its contents."

Liam Stack, for all his professionalism, simply smirked and nodded his head, "I will endeavor to do so sir - but that may be a very long time."

Nodding his head, "You're probably right. When you can, please leave it in her office, so there is at least a waste bin nearby."

Liam chuckled and accepted the letter. "Consider it done, Doctor Kane. Let me show you to your coach."

Walking out into the main courtyard, Emilio saw Marisol standing alone. She was looking down the steps that lead to the street. She said nothing as he stood next to her. He wasn't sure what to say or even what could be said. Everything that held her here had been removed. Her time to move on would come soon.

Her stoic expression seemed tired. It was expected. Perhaps silence was for the best. Around them, they could hear the life of the city slow down and night had finally come. The rain clouds had drifted eastward, leaving only the brilliant night sky above with dozen of stars. The stargazing was soon broken up by a voice below.

"Are you Doctor Emilio Kane?"

The speaker was a woman dressed in a Guild uniform. "Yes, that's me."

"I'm here to take you back to Knot's End sir, are you ready to go?" she asked.

Emilio looked at Marisol, but before he could say anything, she took his hand in hers and began walking down the steps. Wordlessly, he followed her and they both stepped into the coach. The door soon closed, and they felt the lull of the coach move forward.

"How long do I have, Doctor?" she asked.

"It's difficult to say. Sometimes, when a Spirit has been avenged, they go to where they need to go immediately. Other times they go on once the body has been laid to rest."

Marisol nodded her head, "In two days, then. Lykos told Mr. Stack the announcement would come out in the morning. There was an accident." She explained. "The body will be inturned in the royal crypts the day after tomorrow. I did not want to wait here until then." She allowed her shoulders to slump, and looked out at the passing city, "I hope you do not mind. I just don't want to be alone when ... when it happens."

Emilio reached over and touched her knee. "I promise you, you will not be alone."

She gave him a sad smile and then squeezed his hand and returned her attention to the window.

The original trip here had been done within 24 hours because it was a state emergency. The trip back was almost twice that. It was mostly non-stop except for food and watering the horse. It was nighttime when they finally arrived back at Knot's End. Of all the people to greet him when the coach door opened, Emilio did not expect to see Wils Fives.

"Doctor Kane," he said, "Welcome ... back?" Wils said as he looked at Emilio's changed appearance. "Are you okay?"

"Uh, thank you Mr. Fives. Yes, I'm fine. Just the cost of doing business. Is everything alright?" Emilio asked cautiously.

Forcing himself not to stare, Wils continued, "Heard up the chain that you saved one of our Guild Brothers and helped recover the bodies of our fallen. One of those was Nema Foal. She was Lina's wife." He gestured at the driver. "She was reported missing during her run. From what we understand, she was one of the drivers killed by those wolf-skinned bastards. If you don't mind, we'd like to hear how it happened," Wils asked.

His amicable tone almost made Emilio think he was speaking to Enik. "Of course, but what I have to say may be uncomfortable to hear."

"We're not a squeamish lot, Doctor Kane," Wils started.

"Oh, I know that beyond a doubt Mr. Fives - but the methods that were employed in that situation were ... um ... You, in particular, might find disagreeable," Emilio said cautiously.

Wils was silent for a moment, but then asked, "Death Magic?"

Lina had already climbed down, and stood next to Wils. "Please, tell me about my Nema and the others," she asked. "I have to know."

Wils took a deep breath and then nodded in agreement.

Emilio looked back at Marisol and relayed the story of the ambush along the road. When he got to the part about the possession, he expected Wil to do or say something rude. Instead, he simply took a deep breath and chewed the inside of his cheek. When he spoke the names of the dead, Wil took out a piece of paper and wrote the names. While he left nothing out, Emilio did not offer a description of those that were killed. He could see the tears in Lina's eyes. He could not leave the woman with a marred image of her wife.

"Thank you, Doctor Kane. The Guild appreciates your service," Wils said and offered his hand.

Nodding his head, he shook the offered hand. "If you'll excuse me, I think it's time for me to sleep in my bed tonight."

"Did you need a ride, Doctor?" Lina asked.

Emilio shook his head. "The offer is appreciated, truly, but I've been in a wagon far too long and it is a beautiful night.

A little walk will do me good, besides you should get some rest as well. Too many long days wear on the soul."

"Carry on Doctor, and good night," Lina said.

"Good night Lina. Good night, Wils," Emilio said as he gathered up his things from the coach and started down the road.

Wils and Lina watched the Necromist walk away. Both noted that he held his hand out as if he was walking with someone, hand in hand. Looking at each, they silently agreed to forget it. There were strange and dangerous things in this world. It was a good thing that Emilio Kane was on their side.

After they departed the town proper, Marisol spoke up, " I don't want to borrow trouble, but are we certain that was the same Wils Five we met a few days ago? Is it possible that was really a creature in disguise?"

Shocked, he looked over at Marisol and shook his head with a laugh. "Gods no! Not tonight, please."

Marisol smiled and looked out into the distance. Not that far away was a familiar blue light, the one that started all of this. She squeezed his hand and continued along the moonlit path.

Emilio's house remained undisturbed in his absence. The door was locked. The larder was still stocked. A few notes had been tacked to his door. He pulled these down and dropped them on his desk as they entered. He would review them in the morning. The shades below remained in their recorded state, unaware that he had been gone for a few days. The Lawsons continued their bickering, and Page continued her interview. It was as if he had never left.

After ensuring everything was as it should be, Emilio made his way to the bedroom. It was still warm, but perhaps opening the window would make it easier to sleep tonight. He flipped open the latch and pushed the window open. A cool breeze rustled through the curtains.

Turning around, he saw Marisol sitting on his bed, looking out the open window at the night sky.

"Don't sleep downstairs tonight. Stay with me, please."

Emilio nodded and slipped his suspenders off his shoulders and walked to the bed. He sat down next to her and pulled off his shoes. It was not a large bed, but it was big enough for the both of them. He lay back and placed his head on the pillow. Marisol shifted and laid down beside him. Her eyes still staring out the window.

Emilio watched her, taking in the beauty of her death mask and all it entailed. He paused and peered past her face and into the Alma. Where there once had been five flowers crowing her head, there were now six. He smiled.

As they were leaving The Barrows, Emilio heard a voice in his head. The protector who stood at the entrance had passed along a message that now made sense.

Each flower represents a time when one is loved and loved in return.

Emilio placed his hand on Marisol's and entwined his fingers with hers.

Both of them turned to look out the window and into the night, appreciating the beauty before them. It was an endless canvas of blacks, blues, and indigos with a spray of twinkling eternal diamonds. For those few moments, the world and everything else seemed thousands of miles away. They were the only two beings that mattered. And only this moment mattered for the both of them.

Even as sleep overtook him, he refused to let her go.

When he awoke in the morning, he could hear nature all around him. His bed was empty.

She was no longer there.

He had not shared his bed with anyone before. There really had never been time for it. His work was lonely, but he accepted that aspect of it a long time ago. But the pain of her absence was different.

It should not affect him like this. He knew this day was coming. He had expected it to come. It was inevitable. But expecting a thing, and experiencing it, was another. The house had always been empty in that regard. But now it really was.

Tears filled his eyes, and he smiled.

The last two days had been filled with just talking. Sharing each other's company. The trip there had seemed like it was a year ago, while the last two days did not feel long enough. He had gone through a harrowing journey, one that changed him in more ways than he could have ever imagined. He never once thought he could care so deeply for a person who was essentially a stranger. Yet, they connected in so many ways. It was not simply a physical attraction, but so much more that was shared.

Sitting up, he cleared his throat and wiped away the tears from his eyes. There was so much to do, but maybe for today, he needed to just take care of himself. Sighing deeply, he smiled at the light and said softly, "Thank you, Marisol."

"You are welcome?" said a familiar voice.

Turning quickly, he was shocked to see Marisol standing in the doorway. Her Spirit had not moved on.

"You! You should be gone now. You should have moved on when the sun rose," Emilio said in disbelief.

"Yet, here I am. I could leave if you want me to?" she teased.

"Gods no, but what happened? When the sun rose, did nothing happen?" he asked.

Walking over, she sat next to him. "I expected something to happen, but when the sun rose, there was nothing. I waited. Eventually, I just got up and let you sleep. Has this ever happened before? She asked.

"No, but…" he said as Marisol took his hand in hers. Looking down, he felt a thousand questions race through his mind, but he pushed them aside at that moment. Gingerly reaching up, he cupped her cheek. She still felt cold, but he could feel her there.

Closing her eyes at the warmth of his touch, Marisol leaned in and lightly kissed his lips.

Touching his forehead to hers, he finished his thought, "…but I'm glad it did."

THE
NECROMIST
&
SANCTIONED
NECROMATIC
UNDERSTANDING

A Discipline, Trade,
and the Understanding of Styx's Blessing

Foreward by
Eunice Fountains

FUGUE ACADEMY TEXT

INTERACTIONS

The dead cannot normally interact with the living unless they fully manifested themselves. Manifestation is rare for Shades, but possible for Spirits. However, the process of manifestation is emotionally taxing for the Spirit - so much that it leaves the Spirit susceptible to those darker emotions (Sorrow, Fear & Anger). So while it is possible to interact with the physical world while manifested - such acts can lead to a darker path.

Interaction on any level is a matter that needs to be fully considered by the Necromist. While there are various rites at our disposal, one must ask themselves the following:

- What benefit does the interaction provide to the Departed?
- Is there any danger to yourself or your current environment?
- Is the interaction necessary for them to move on?
- How have you prepared yourself for the interaction (benign and hostile)

SOUL CORRUPTION

A Spirit overtaken by its emotions became a warped reflection of its last emotions.

Those who died with sorrow or despair were known as Howlers. Their mournful wail could cause depression and hopelessness to flourish in a person to the point of taking their own life - thus creating more howlers in the process.

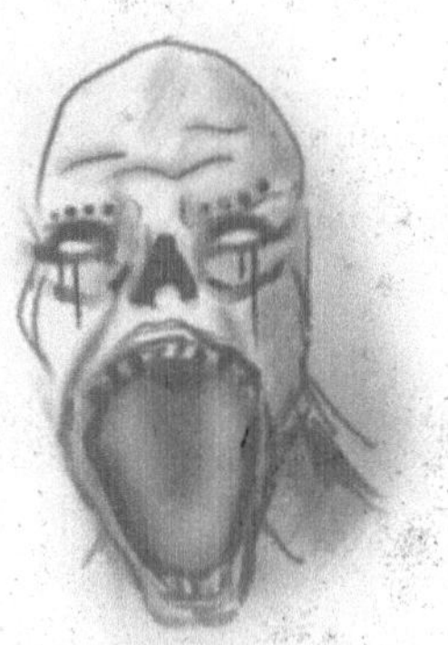

Those who died of fear or terror were known as Screamers. It is sort of a misnomer as these beings are never actually heard. The expression of terror is so frightening that when they manifest - it can cause a person to faint or die right on the spot. Those that die this way will more than likely come back as Screamers themselves.

Those who died of rage or anger are known as the Wrathful. Their emotions create a physical manifestation in the real world - otherworldly cold and the ability to physically interact with real-world - while they don't propagate like the others, they can cause waves of destruction and death for those unfortunate to be in their way.

AFTERWORD

It started with a picture.

It came across Charm's feed one morning and she was taken by it. Something told her–buy this cover from Etheric, NOW. She sent the image to Tony and said, "So, I have an idea..." Chewing on the concept, Tony took a shower with that Kate Bush song playing loudly. You know the one. Less than thirty minutes later, we had a blurb, character concepts, and a new piece of cover art. It wasn't our current project(s), but we didn't care. Suddenly, there was a whole new story and a whole new world being developed right before our eyes. It was brilliant and amazing, and we loved it.

We never know where our inspiration will come from next. We only know that when it does ... it's time to listen.

We hope you enjoyed this little jaunt with Dr. Kane and Marisol, and we hope to see you again soon.

Tony & Charm

P.S. The best way to thank an author Is with a review. We'd love to hear from you.

https://tinyurl.com/RaiseTheDeadReview

ABOUT AUTHORS

SandDancer Publications

C.S. Kading and Tony Fuentes have been working together and crafting stories for over two decades. Partners in both mischief and memories, this dynamic duo combines real-world experience with formal education, to bring you stories to tickle your imagination and delight your hearts.

SandDancer was born out of the pandemic and a need to stay sane. We could not enjoy the company of others beyond the safety of our bubble, so we came to you the only other way we could - through books and storytelling.

Tony Fuentes
Literary Titan Gold Award-Winning Author
Tony is Renaissance Man in Geek's clothing; not only an author with a weird imagination, but also a painter, gamer, and part-time occultist. With his writing, he tries to spin humor into the world's grounded reality. At the same, he tries to get the audience to look into the stars and dream

further beyond. In all things, he strives to give the weird and the wondrous things a place in the world for all to enjoy.

- B.S. COMM

- IASFA

- indie B.R.A.G. Medallion recipient

C.S. Kading

Literary Titan Gold Award-Winning Author
Poet, playwright, and storyteller, whose love for writing began in 3rd grade when she won a district writing contest. Her love for fantastical forces motivates her to create stories of heroes, villains, gods, and monsters that often have a foundation in Old World mythology and legends.

- Member: IASFA, IAN

- MAED

- indie B.R.A.G. Medallion recipient

ALSO BY

Check out our works on our website:

SandDancer Publications
https://sanddancer.pub/

<u>The World of Sanctum Series</u>
Epic Fantasy

Sanctum: Sands of Setesh

Sanctum: Forests of Avalon

Longest Night: A Sanctum Tale

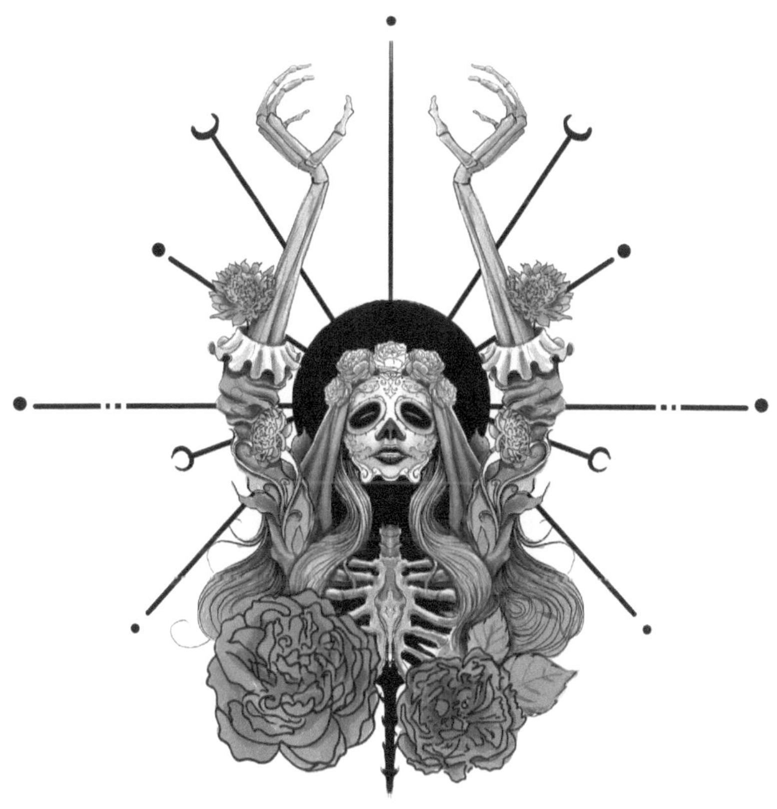